S0-ACP-337

TRUE BLUE K-9 UNIT: BROOKLYN CHRISTMAS

LAURA SCOTT
MAGGIE K. BLACK

LOVE INSPIRED SUSPENSE

INSPIRATIONAL ROMANCE

If you purchased this book without a cover you should be aware
that this book is stolen property. It was reported as "unsold and
destroyed" to the publisher, and neither the author nor the
publisher has received any payment for this "stripped book."

Special thanks and acknowledgment are given to
Laura Scott and Maggie K. Black for their contributions
to the True Blue K-9 Unit: Brooklyn miniseries.

LOVE INSPIRED® SUSPENSE
INSPIRATIONAL ROMANCE

Recycling programs
for this product may
not exist in your area.

ISBN-13: 978-1-335-57474-9

True Blue K-9 Unit: Brooklyn Christmas

Copyright © 2020 by Harlequin Books S.A.

Holiday Stalker
Copyright © 2020 by Harlequin Books S.A.

Gift-Wrapped Danger
Copyright © 2020 by Harlequin Books S.A.

All rights reserved. No part of this book may be used or reproduced in
any manner whatsoever without written permission except in the case of
brief quotations embodied in critical articles and reviews.

This is a work of fiction. Names, characters, places and incidents are either the
product of the author's imagination or are used fictitiously. Any resemblance to
actual persons, living or dead, businesses, companies, events or locales is entirely
coincidental.

This edition published by arrangement with Harlequin Books S.A.

For questions and comments about the quality of this book, please contact us
at CustomerService@Harlequin.com.

Love Inspired
22 Adelaide St. West, 40th Floor
Toronto, Ontario M5H 4E3, Canada
www.Harlequin.com

Printed in U.S.A.

Meet the officers of the
True Blue K-9 Unit: Brooklyn series
and their brave K-9 partners

Officer: Max Santelli

K-9 Partner: Sam the rottweiler

Assignment: Keep tech specialist Eden Chang safe and figure out who's after her.

Officer: Noelle Orton

K-9 Partner: Liberty the Labrador retriever

Assignment: Work with Adam Jolly to find out who is hiding drugs in the toys for his Christmas toy drive.

Laura Scott is a nurse by day and an author by night. She has always loved romance and read faith-based books by Grace Livingston Hill in her teenage years. She's thrilled to have published over twenty-five books for Love Inspired Suspense. She has two adult children and lives in Milwaukee, Wisconsin, with her husband of over thirty years. Please visit Laura at laurascottbooks.com, as she loves to hear from her readers.

Maggie K. Black is an award-winning journalist and romantic suspense author with an insatiable love of traveling the world. She has lived in the American South, Europe and the Middle East. She now makes her home in Canada with her history-teacher husband, their two beautiful girls and a small but mighty dog. Maggie enjoys connecting with her readers at maggiekblack.com.

CONTENTS

CONTENTS

HOLIDAY STALKER

Laura Scott

This book is dedicated to all my fellow continuity authors, Heather Woodhaven, Lenora Worth, Terri Reed, Valerie Hansen, Sharon Dunn, Dana Mentink, Shirlee McCoy and Maggie K. Black. Thanks for being a joy to work with!

Fear thou not; for I am with thee: be not dismayed;
for I am thy God: I will strengthen thee;
yea, I will help thee; yea, I will uphold thee
with the right hand of my righteousness.
—Isaiah 41:10

ONE

Eden Chang hunched her shoulders and
tucked her chin beneath the neckline of her
bright red winter coat. Shivering in the cold
dark night, she quickened her pace toward
the Bay Ridge Avenue subway entrance.

A scattering of fat fluffy snowflakes
began to fall, bringing the promised white
Christmas the meteorologists had pre-
dicted. Wreaths decorated the light posts
with holiday cheer. Normally she loved
snow, and the Christmas holiday, but not
tonight.

Not when she was being followed.

Eden pressed a hand to her abdomen,
holding the computer bag in place. She'd
looped the strap over her shoulder beneath
her coat. Resisting the urge to look over
her shoulder, she walked faster. Her senses

were on full alert, the hair on the back of her neck standing upright in alarm. The sooner she could get near crowds of people, the safer she'd feel.

Lord, please guide me to safety.

At the entrance leading down to the subway station, she hesitated. Should she risk turning around and go back to the mostly deserted Brooklyn K-9 Unit police station? Or take the subway to head home the way she'd planned? As the technical specialist for the Brooklyn K-9 Unit, she knew the subways had dozens of cameras, more so than what you could count on being available out on the street.

Since their precinct happened to be a good six blocks away, and her train would be arriving shortly, she decided to head down to the subway. She quickly pushed through the turnstile. The area was well lit, the brightness making her squint. Seeing a small group of what she thought might be college students standing near one of the green pillars, she immediately walked toward them, hoping the mere proximity of others would scare off the guy trailing her.

If only she'd gotten a better glimpse of his face. Dressed in black, with a dark cap covering his hair, and the collar of his black leather coat flipped up and hiding most of his face, she couldn't say for sure who he was. She'd first noticed him about two blocks after leaving work but hadn't thought much about it until she'd caught another glimpse of him still behind her on the next block. She'd taken a brief detour, thinking she'd lose him, but didn't.

There was no reason for anyone to follow her, yet she felt certain the guy behind her was Tayron Lee, a friend of her older brother, Ricky. Tayron, who preferred to be called *Tiger* and often called her brother *Rat*, gave her the creeps.

Eden stood near the college students, glancing up at the camera mounted between the ceiling and the wall, before scanning the faces of the pedestrians coming through the turnstile and into the subway. So far, there was no sign of Tayron, or any other man dressed from head to toe in black. Holding her phone in her hand, she silently urged the train to arrive. When she heard the sound of its approach, her shoulders slumped with relief.

Finally! She moved away from the students, turning to watch as the train slowed to a stop. Several people were standing near the doorway, waiting to come off, so she stepped back to give them room.

A blur of movement caught the corner of her eye. She whirled around in time to see a dark figure jabbing his gloved hand toward her abdomen. The light bounced off something shiny.

A knife!

Before she could move or scream, the blade went deep through the puffy fabric of her coat, hitting the computer bag hidden underneath. For a moment the man seemed surprised at her non-reaction, then he jerked the knife out and instantly spun away, running back through the turnstile and up the stairs to the street.

"Help! Stop him! He tried to stab me!" Eden found her voice, shouting above the din.

The college students gaped at her while several other pedestrians looked around in confusion. A tall man with dark hair wearing a NYPD uniform and jacket came barreling out of the train, holding the leash of a tall black-and-gold dog wearing a K-9 vest.

"Where did he go?" Maxwell Santelli, one of the transit officers from her K-9 precinct, lightly grasped her arm. "Are you okay?"

"I'm fine, the knife hit my bag, but he headed up the stairs to the street. Hurry!"

"Stay here and wait for me. Come, Sam." Max didn't waste another second and ran after her attacker.

Eden was conscious of the numerous people gawking at her. She glanced down at her coat, wondering if she had actually been hit, but thankfully there was no blood.

The one-inch tear in her coat was the only evidence of the knife attack. Fingering the tear, she sent up a silent prayer, thanking God for protecting her.

When she glanced up again, she realized several people were still staring at her.

"I have a computer bag under my coat," she announced to no one in particular. "The tip of the knife hit my bag. I'm fine, but my computer may not be."

A couple of people let out nervous laughs. Others looked relieved. One kid was using his phone to take a video.

She scowled. "Turn that off."

The kid returned her gaze defiantly for a long second before slinking away.

The seconds ticked by slowly as she waited for K-9 officer Max Santelli and his Rottweiler, Sam, to return. The fact that they were working late surprised her. Was there some sort of case he was dealing with that she wasn't aware of? It would be unusual since she was the one with the ability to tap in to view all the security cameras, including those on the subways.

Max. She shivered, only this time not from the cold. Of all the cops within their K-9 unit close enough to respond, why did it have to be him? Max Santelli was tall and muscular with dark hair, light blue eyes and a dimple that flashed in his left cheek when he smiled.

Which frankly wasn't often. Of all the

cops she worked with, Max was the most reserved and serious of the group.

And far too attractive for her peace of mind.

"Eden?"

She jerked her gaze up to meet Max's. "Did you find him?"

He grimaced and shook his head. "No, sorry." His gaze dropped to the tear in her coat, a frown furrowing his brow. "You're sure you're not hurt?"

"I had my computer bag beneath my coat."

"You always carry your computer bag under your coat?" Max took a moment to examine the tear made by the knife blade.

"Yes. I have very expensive equipment and this way it makes it harder to steal." She didn't bring her work home, that would be against the rules, but being a computer geek, she always had the most expensive and up-to-date technology. She liked using her computer on her lunch break and wasn't about to let it get ripped off by some low-life.

"I'm glad the blade didn't cut you."

She nodded, but suddenly felt overwhelmed by the near miss. Her knees threatened to buckle, so she staggered over to the nearby bench and sat down, trying to understand what had just happened.

She hadn't just been followed, which was bad enough; she'd been stabbed. Why? Who would want to hurt her? Even Tayron, creepy as he was—with his knowing, leering grin—hadn't ever given her the impression he wanted to kill her. He'd made it clear he wanted to date her, so why stab her?

"Easy now, take a deep breath in and let it out slowly."

Max's mesmerizing voice broke into her troubled thoughts and she found herself following his advice. He dropped into the seat beside her, wrapping his arm around her shoulders. "Sam, Heel," Max commanded. The Rottweiler came over and dropped to his haunches beside them.

The urge to lean against Max, absorbing his strength, was strong. She had to take several deep breaths before she could speak. "Thanks for coming to the rescue."

"Can you tell me what happened?" Max's tone was low, gruff yet gentle at the same time. His nearness was distracting, his sandalwood scent strong, but she did her best to concentrate on providing the information he needed.

"I felt someone following me for the past few blocks and debated whether to return to the precinct or keep going."

"Why were you working so late? It's past ten thirty at night," Max interrupted.

"Why are you here this late?" She couldn't hide the exasperation in her voice.

"There's been a rash of subway robberies," Max admitted. "I was approved for some overtime."

She nodded, belatedly remembering that. "I have a lot of video I've been asked to review and it took longer than I thought. The point is, I knew someone was behind me on the street, but I didn't expect him to follow me down into the subway station and stab me."

"I know." Max's arm around her shoulders tightened for a moment before he moved away. He shifted on the bench to face her. "Did you recognize him?"

She hesitated and tried to bring the glimpse of the man's face into her mind's eye. Had it been Tayron? The collar and black scarf had hidden a good portion of his face. She couldn't even say for sure what race he was. Tayron was Chinese, like her and her brother, and the only one she could imagine doing something like this, but to be fair, she'd been distracted by the knife. By the time she'd lifted her gaze to his face, the attacker had been turning away.

"Not yet, but I'm sure I will once I have a chance to examine the subway video more closely."

"That sounds to me like you have a suspect who you think did this."

She sighed and grimaced. "Just a possibility. Tayron Lee is a friend of my older brother's. He's asked me out nonstop for the past year, used to show up at my apartment building until I moved six weeks ago. I wondered if he was the one following me. But to stab me with a knife? That's extreme, even for him."

"Tayron Lee," Max repeated. His serious expression didn't reveal his thoughts. "Anyone else? Other secret admirers? Former boyfriends?"

"No." She briefly considered her three male friends from college. The four of them called themselves the Geek Quad, but couldn't imagine one of her longtime friends turning on her. And none of the guys had ever asked her out. "I can't imagine anyone doing something like this."

"Keep thinking about it. You may remember something else." Max fell silent for a moment, then added, "I'd like to review the video with you."

"Sure." He was, after all, the responding officer. She blew out a sigh. "Tomorrow will be soon enough. I'm not sure I'm up to looking at it now."

"I'll escort you home." Max stood and Sam sprang to his feet, too. "After giving the all clear for the train to resume."

He used his radio to communicate the information, then put his hand beneath Eden's elbow as she rose to her feet.

"That's not necessary. I'll be fine."

"Humor me." When she nodded, he put a hand beneath her elbow. "Let's go."

Powerless to resist, she allowed Max to lead her onto the train. There was only one empty seat and he steered her toward it, choosing to stand before her, with Sam at his side.

The Rottweiler was beautiful with his black-and-gold coloring, but he was a working dog, so she didn't try to pet him. Yet she couldn't help but smile at the idea of Sam meeting Charlie, her roommate Anna's orange tabby cat.

"Where do you live?"

She shifted the bulky computer beneath her coat to a more comfortable position, then glanced up at him. "Sunset Park. I share a two-bedroom apartment with a friend."

He nodded. "That's good. I'm glad you won't be alone."

"Yeah, well, I am living alone for the next two weeks. Anna is skiing in Colorado with her family through the New Year." It was part of the reason she'd chosen to work late. No sense rushing home to an empty apartment.

Max scowled. "Do you have somewhere else you can stay for tonight?"

She thought again of her three computer geek friends. Darnell Hicks, Tom Gellner and Bryon Avery. As much as they'd hung out in high school and college, gaming or surfing the net, honing their hacking skills, they weren't the kind of guys she wanted to ask this kind of personal favor from. They were friends, but she didn't want to live with any of them, even temporarily. "No. I'll be fine." She put on a brave face, even though she was nervous about being alone. Charlie the tabby would be there, but he wasn't protective the way Sam and Max were.

Weariness washed over her. Being recruited by the NYPD during college because of her technical skills had been exciting, the perfect way to honor her father, Kent Chang, a cop who'd served New York City for over twenty years before dying of cancer when she and Ricky were in college. Her mother, Louise, had died a year later, from what Eden privately believed was a broken heart.

But working as the technical specialist for the Brooklyn K-9 Unit didn't mean she was fighting crime on the front lines. Being in danger wasn't something she was accustomed to, preferring to work behind the scenes in order to bring the bad guys to justice.

It was officers like Max, and the others, who put their lives on the line every day.

"Oh, this is my stop." She was about to reach for the pole, but Max caught her hand and helped her up. He held her hand for a moment longer than he needed to and then cupped her elbow as they left the subway.

"Which way?" Max asked when they reached the street level.

"To the right." The neighborhood where she and Anna lived wasn't the best, but it wasn't the worst. Much better than what they'd had before, thanks to Anna's parents helping them. "I hope I'm not taking you too far out of your way."

"You're not." Max didn't let on where he

lived, and despite her curiosity, she didn't push.

When they reached her building, she expected him to leave her at the front door, but he and Sam followed her inside. They took the elevator to the second floor of the three-story building.

"This way," she said, turning toward the apartment she shared with Anna. As she was about to put her key in the lock, Sam forced his way in front of her and sat directly by the door, his gaze locked on some imaginary spot. She glanced down at the K-9 in surprise. "What is he doing?"

"Stay back." Max put his arm out to prevent her from going any farther. "Sam is alerting on the door."

"Alerting why?"

Max's gaze was grim. "He's trained to sniff out bombs."

Bombs? The floor undulated beneath her feet, and she reached out to brace herself against the wall. First the stabbing attempt and now this? A possible bomb?

What did it all mean?

TWO

Max hated knowing Eden Chang was in the middle of danger. Not only was Eden a member of the Brooklyn K-9 Unit family but there was the added issue of the way he'd been distracted by her beauty over the past few months, more times than he cared to count.

An attraction he had no intention of acting on. Losing his fiancée, Jessica, in an auto accident last year had shaken him to the core. A year later, he still wasn't ready for another relationship.

Still, he was thankful he'd been on the subway in time to rush to Eden's rescue. It galled him that the attacker had gotten away. Sam was a great tracker, and skilled bomb-sniffing dog. If the guy had left something behind, he felt certain they would have caught up to him.

"Come, Sam." He wanted his partner far away from any potential explosion. But as they made their way through the hallway, he was somewhat reassured that Sam didn't alert at any other apartment doors. He used the radio clipped to his collar and asked for the bomb squad to be sent to her building.

He glanced at Eden. "Who has a key to your place? Your brother?"

"No way. I wouldn't trust him and he's never been here." She frowned. "No one else has a key except my roommate, Anna."

Max swept his gaze over the area. There was no sign of anything out of place in the hallway. Sam had alerted only in front of her door. Did that mean someone had come up here, tried to get in and left? Sam had an incredible nose; he would alert at the faintest hint of oil from an explosive device.

Had the guy from the subway come here first to look for Eden? Had he tested the door, leaving trace oil behind? The thought made his blood run cold. "We need to get out of here."

"But—Charlie, Anna's tabby cat, is in there." Eden's dark eyes were wide with fear. Petite in stature, she was incredibly beautiful with her silky long straight dark hair framing her face and he had to swallow hard to keep himself from babbling like an idiot.

No distractions, remember?

"We can't risk it." He put his hand beneath Eden's elbow. "Come on, we'll wait to see what the bomb squad thinks."

They took the stairs down to the lobby level. The bomb squad arrived within minutes. The officer in charge took Eden's key and immediately requested an evacuation of the building before heading upstairs to enter Eden's apartment.

Max took Eden outside, keeping her close within the crowd. As more and more people gathered around them, he found himself wondering if someone was out there right now watching, waiting for a chance to get at Eden.

If so, they'd have to get past him and Sam first.

After a long hour, the bomb squad called an all clear.

"We didn't find anything in your apartment or anywhere else." The guy in charge returned Eden's key. "There was trace oil on the door handle that must have caused your K-9 to alert."

"I guess that's good news." Her voice was faint, as if she were hanging on by a thread.

The local cops who'd responded along with the bomb squad came over to question Eden. When she explained about the subway attack, Max readily corroborated her story.

"Anything else?" the officer asked.

He turned toward Eden. "Do you know if your brother's friend, Tayron Lee, has ever played around with making bombs?"

"Never." Eden's response came without hesitation. "He might be obsessed with asking me out, but creating a bomb? Trying to stab me? That just doesn't sound like him."

"Anyone else fit the pattern?"

"No." Eden looked defeated. "Fortunately, Tayron is the only one I've had issues with on a personal level."

The officers exchanged a glance. "We'll question him."

"Thanks." The idea of Tayron harassing her was concerning. Even if he wasn't responsible for the stabbing or leaving the smear of explosive oil behind, Max would love nothing more than to toss the guy in jail for simply being a jerk.

Normally, a guy trying to get a woman to notice him wouldn't attack her.

On the other hand, a person with behavioral health issues could become obsessed and unbalanced enough to lash out at the woman he coveted. Which might include stabbing and making bombs. Was it possible Tayron Lee fell into the latter category?

"By the way, he likes to call himself *Tiger*." Eden's wry tone had him lifting a brow.

"Why?"

She shook her head. "No clue. I guess maybe because he identifies with the animal. He calls my brother, Ricky, *Rat*."

That was weird, and he wondered about possible gang connections. The patrol officers took down that information, as well.

After the local police and the bomb squad members had left the scene, he and Sam escorted Eden back upstairs to her apartment. It was well past midnight by now and as she unlocked her door, he put a hand on her arm. "I don't want you staying here alone tonight."

She grimaced. "I'll be fine. I'm sure the bomb squad wouldn't have cleared my apartment if there was a threat."

"It's not just the bomb scare, Eden. That knife attack was a close call. Would you mind if Sam and I bunked on the sofa?"

There was a brief flash of hope in her eyes, but then she shook her head. "I have Charlie the tabby cat here, remember? I don't think Sam will appreciate sharing the space with a cat."

"He'll be fine, and I'll rest better knowing you're protected." He turned to his K-9 and bent over to rub his ears for a moment. After she unlocked the door, he led Sam inside. Eden followed behind them.

Sam's nose worked as they made their way into the kitchen and living room. A fully decorated Christmas tree was tucked into the corner with a baby gate around it, the lights brightening the space. A loud meow echoed from up ahead and an orange ball of fur barreled past him.

"Woof, woof!" Sam let out two deep-throated barks.

"No. Be quiet." His tone was one Sam knew to obey. "Heel."

Sam dropped to his haunches but swiveled his black-and-tan head around, his nose sniffing the air to track the feline.

"No," he commanded. Sam glanced at him balefully.

"Maybe they'll make friends soon." She offered a wry smile. After double locking the apartment door, she turned to face him. "Thank you, Max. You and Sam staying here like this is going well above and beyond the call of duty."

Her gratitude made him feel embarrassed. "It's not a big deal. You know we always take care of our own."

Her gaze clung to his for a moment before she turned away. After shedding her coat, she took the computer bag strap off over her head and set it on the table. He'd noticed Eden always dressed in dark slacks with brightly colored blouses. Today's was a deep vibrant blue. "Who would have thought my paranoia of being robbed would help save my life?"

"Yeah." The close call still bothered him. "I need to take Sam out one last time, would you mind lending me your keys so I can get in and out of the building?"

"Sure." She dropped them into his palm. "I'll leave a pillow and blanket on the sofa for you."

"Thanks." Max let himself out, taking care to lock the door behind him, then took Sam outside. There was a small grassy area not far from the apartment building. He couldn't stop thinking about the knife attack and Sam alerting outside Eden's door. Logically, it would seem that the attacker had initially checked her apartment, then set out to find Eden at the precinct. To his mind, there wasn't enough time to get from the subway back to Eden's place before he and Sam had escorted her home.

Unless, of course, there was more than one person involved. The instant the thought entered his mind he rejected it. His gut told him this type of attack was one man's obsession, maybe rooted in a deep need for control.

Tayron Lee? Or someone else? Eden claimed she didn't have any old boyfriends, but he found that difficult to believe. Eden was beautiful, smart and friendly to everyone within the Brooklyn K-9 Unit.

No, it was far more likely she was friends with some guy who admired her from afar. Someone who wanted more from Eden.

Someone a little like him. Max rolled his eyes and shook his head. No way. He wasn't obsessed or imbalanced. And he'd worked hard to keep his admiration of Eden to himself. No one in their unit knew how he truly felt about her.

And Max vowed to keep it that way. Loving someone and losing them was the most painful experience he'd gone through.

He didn't plan to risk his heart like that again.

Eden placed a folded blanket and one of her spare pillows on the sofa, then began searching for Charlie. Anna's tabby wasn't the friendliest cat on the planet, and he couldn't be happy to have a Rottweiler invading his space.

"Charlie? Come on, Charlie, I have a treat for you." She held out the bit of tuna that normally worked like a charm to coax the feline out of hiding.

Not this time. She searched under the beds and behind the sofa without success. She even checked the Christmas tree, which Charlie generally ignored thanks to the baby gate they used to protect it. When she heard the locks on the front door, she carried the tuna back to the kitchen where Charlie's food and water dish were located. Maybe the cat would come out later to snatch up his treat.

"Hi." She was ridiculously nervous at having Max and Sam in the apartment, even though she trusted them with her life. It was her own stupid awareness of Max that kept tripping her up. "Um, I wanted to let you know that I need to be in to work early tomorrow, so I'm hoping to leave here by six thirty."

He looked a bit surprised but nodded. "That's not a problem. We'll go in together. That way we can review the camera footage first thing."

She was glad she wouldn't be riding the subway alone, even if that meant spending more time with Max. She forced a smile. "Great. Well, good night, then."

"Good night, Eden."

Max's low husky voice echoed over and over in her mind, following her in her dreams. His presence must have helped keep the nightmares at bay, because in spite of the nerve-racking events of the night before, she slept better than expected, waking up to a loud meow in her ear.

Prying an eye open, she found Charlie's nose mere inches from her face. He meowed again and batted at her, letting her know of his displeasure.

"Hey, don't yell at me. I offered tuna as an apology." Great, now she was talking to the cat. She scrambled from the bed and quickly got ready for work. After choosing a bright purple blouse and sweater, she added matching globe-shaped ornament earrings in an effort to cheer herself up. She was determined not to let this situation ruin her favorite holiday. By the time she entered the kitchen, Charlie had disappeared again, no doubt hiding from Sam.

She stopped short when she found Max cooking eggs on the stove. "Good morning." Had that high squeaky voice really come from her?

"Morning. Hope you don't mind, but I worked later than planned and didn't eat dinner last night. I was hungry and decided to cook breakfast. Although I couldn't find any coffee."

"Oh, sorry, I prefer green tea. And of course I don't mind you making breakfast." She squelched a flash of guilt that he missed dinner because of her.

"I already took Sam out, but I need to get him some food, too." He flipped the eggs, making them over easy, then met her gaze. "I live close by, but there's plenty of dog food at the training center, so we can just head to the precinct."

"You live in Sunset Park?" Again with the squeaky voice? Honestly, she needed to get a grip. "If you want to go to your place, that's fine. I should have thought about getting food for Sam last night."

"That's nice of you, but he'll be fine until we get to the precinct. He's not the one who missed dinner." He pulled out a plate and used the spatula to move the eggs from the pan, then added two slices of freshly buttered toast. "How do you like your eggs?"

"Um, over easy is fine." No man had ever cooked breakfast for her, mainly because she hadn't dated anyone seriously since her freshman year of college. Gregory had rudely broken her heart, making a fool of her among his friends, and she'd never fully trusted her taste in men from that point forward.

It was easier to remain alone.

"Here." Max set the plate in front of her. "Mine will be ready in a minute. Eat before it gets cold."

She took a moment to bow her head, silently giving thanks for the food, then dug in. "These are delicious, thanks."

"They're just eggs." He shrugged off her gratitude, but the dimple in his left cheek flashed in a brief smile. The smile transformed his features, making him even more good-looking.

She was almost finished with her eggs when Max dropped into the chair across from her with his own plate. "How long have you lived here?"

"In Sunset Park? Just six weeks, but before that Anna and I lived in Dyker Heights. We've been living together since I graduated from college, roughly six years ago."

"Six?" He looked at her in surprise. "You look too young to have been out of college that long."

"I skipped a year." She shrugged it off as no big deal. "I was one of four who received a special technical scholarship from high school. I had enough credits to go in as a sophomore, and the NYPD recruited me shortly thereafter."

"Impressive." The admiration in his gaze made her blush.

"Not really, my friends were recruited by bigger agencies. Darnell Hicks landed a job with the FBI, Tom Gellner, the CIA and Bryon Avery, the NSA." She grinned. "We call ourselves the Geek Quad."

The dimple in his left cheek flashed again. "Why do I think you were also offered a job with the FBI, the CIA or the NSA?"

Her blush deepened and she quickly rose to her feet and carried her dirty dishes to the sink. "I was, but I wanted to work with the NYPD." She decided not to mention the fact that she'd been contacted by a federal government recruiter again just a week ago. They wanted her to reconsider working within one of their agencies, even offered to double her current salary. It was an honor to be considered for such a prestigious position, but she wasn't sure she was ready to leave her job with the Brooklyn K-9 Unit. She glanced at him over her shoulder. "My father, Kent Chang, was a police officer for twenty years. He loved fighting crime for this city, but cancer took him when I was eighteen."

"I'm sorry to hear that." Max's tenderness made her throat swell with emotion.

"I'm sure that was difficult for you and your brother."

"It was." Ricky had gone a little wild afterward, which she partially blamed on Tayron Lee. "But I feel like working for the NYPD and now with the Brooklyn K-9 Unit is my way of honoring my father's memory."

Max nodded thoughtfully. "Understandable."

She stacked the dirty dishes, cleaning up a bit as Max finished his eggs. At six fifteen, they were bundled in their winter gear, her computer bag hidden beneath her coat once again, and on their way.

"You okay with taking the subway?" Max glanced at her with concern.

"Yes." No way would she allow the stabbing to prevent her from using the subway to get to work. Rideshares were expensive.

Max stayed close at her side. The wind was brisk, but the snow had stopped falling at some point during the night.

The subway ride back to Bay Ridge was uneventful and despite the early hour, the train was packed, making idle conversation difficult. Which was okay with her, because she had no idea how to make small talk with Max.

"Any word on Tayron?" she asked, when they made their way to the precinct.

"Not yet." Max scowled. "I spoke to Officer Clayborn earlier this morning. They're looking for Tayron, just to talk to him as a person of interest."

"The video may clear him," she felt compelled to point out.

"Maybe. But the attacker could be someone Tayron knows." They arrived at the limestone building that housed the K-9 Unit, Max holding the door open for her.

The front-desk clerk, Penny MacGregor, was already seated when they walked in. "Hi, Eden, Max."

"Hi, Penny." Eden was glad to see Penny was smiling. The young woman had been so much happier since her parents' murderer had been brought to justice recently and K-9 Detective Tyler Walker had proposed marriage.

Max smiled at Penny. "Has the rest of the team arrived yet? Your brother, maybe?"

Penny's brother, Bradley MacGregor, was a detective with the K-9 Unit.

"Not yet. Bradley's actually out picking up coffee, and I expect everyone else to start trickling in soon," Penny answered.

Max nodded and turned toward Eden. "I need to take Sam to the training center. Wait for me before going through the video from last night, okay?"

"I'll bring it up and have it ready." She didn't want to wait, but understood Sam needed food and water.

"Oh, before you go, Eden, there was a package for you when I came in this morning," Penny said.

She froze, the tiny hairs standing up on the back of her neck. "What kind of package?"

"A box addressed to you from Secret Santa." Penny reached beneath the desk and brought up the small square box wrapped innocuously enough with brown paper. "I didn't think we were doing the Secret Santa thing this year."

"We're not." She made no move to take it. "There's no return address."

Sam whined and pushed between them to sit directly in front of the desk.

The same way he had at her apartment door last night.

"Everyone out." Max didn't hesitate. "We need to evacuate the building."

"What's going on?" Penny asked, coming out from behind the desk.

"Sam is alerting on the package." He ushered her and Penny outside. "Are you sure no one else is here?"

"I'm—sure. I just opened and unlocked the door ten minutes ago." Penny's voice shook.

Max used his radio to call the bomb squad once again.

"You better let Sarge know." Eden finally found her voice. "Especially if it's related to the stabbing."

"Stabbing?" Penny's voice rose in agitation.

"I'll fill you in later." Max shrugged out of his coat and offered it to Penny, who slipped it on gratefully.

Eden stared through the glass doorway

at the small square box still sitting innocuously on Penny's desk.

Who on earth would send her a bomb? And why?

THREE

For the second time in less than twelve hours, Eden watched the bomb squad arrive. Minutes later, Gavin Sutherland pulled up, the tall dark-haired sergeant's grim expression appearing to be carved from granite.

"Max, fill me in."

Eden listened as Max explained about the knife attack at the subway station, and how his K-9 partner, Sam, had alerted on Eden's apartment door and again, here in front of the Secret Santa package.

"You have a theory?" Gavin asked.

"Yes." Max glanced at her, then back to their boss. "I believe the guy who stabbed her must have been working with bombs at some point and still had oil lingering on his fingertips when he checked out Eden's apartment."

"You think there's a bomb in the package left for Eden?" Penny asked, her eyes wide.

"Maybe." Max blew on his cupped hands in an effort to keep warm. "We'll know soon enough."

"We have the bomb secured," someone from the bomb squad called out. "Looks like an explosive device was hidden in a snow globe. We have it in a container for transport."

Eden went still. She collected snow globes of various shapes and sizes. A personal fact that a stranger wouldn't know. The gift had to have been sent by someone who knew her personally.

"If you can get prints, let us know," Gavin directed. "And I want the building cleared before we head back inside."

"I'll take Sam," Max offered. "Seek, Sam. Seek!"

Swallowing her instinctive protest, Eden reminded herself that Max and Sam had a job to do. Their recently established Brooklyn K-9 Unit was housed in a beautiful limestone three-story building, which had been the former home of another police precinct that had outgrown the space and moved into a larger building. Adjacent to the unit was another structure housing the K-9 training center and kennels. It was upsetting to know that the one place she'd always felt safe had been tainted with a bomb.

This guy had gone too far.

Max and Sam returned fifteen minutes later. "All clear."

"Good." Gavin took the lead heading back inside. Eden and Penny followed. "I want a staff meeting within the hour."

"Will do," Penny said, returning Max's jacket, then resuming her post behind the desk. "I'll call everyone in."

"I need to review the subway video," Eden said to Max. "Maybe we can learn something before the meeting."

"I know." His voice was gentle, the way it had been last night. His kindness helped keep her grounded. "I'll get Sam taken care of at the kennels and join you as soon as possible."

With a terse nod, she turned away and headed to the third floor of the precinct where her workspace was located.

Still shaken by the snow-globe bomb intended for her, she forced herself to get to work. She had several stacked computer screens at her workstation, and her desk was one that could raise and lower so she could sit or stand behind it.

She pulled up the footage from the front of the precinct. The same man dressed in black could be seen coming up to the station, carrying a small brown package, leaving a minute later. He kept his head down, his coat collar hiding his face. The drop-off had taken place less than two minutes after she left. Suppressing a chill, she then pulled the subway video from the past twelve hours as Max joined her.

He came up to stand behind her, leaning over her shoulder to see the video, making her conscious of her petite stature. Her head barely reached his chin. "Are you starting with the attack?"

"No, I viewed the front door of the station first. See?" She gestured to one of the screens. "You can see he drops off the package but there's no good view of his face."

"I don't like it."

"I know. This screen—" she gestured to the next one over "—has the video up from the subway station. I didn't go back to find the guy dressed in black, because it seems obvious now he knew where I was headed as I left the precinct."

"I hope we find him." Max's sandalwood scent seemed to surround her as she played the video from two different camera angles, each displayed on their own screen. She slowed the video down when she caught a glimpse of her cheerful red coat.

For long moments neither of them spoke, their eyes glued to the screen. When a figure dressed in black came through the turnstile, she hit the pause button.

"That's him." Her voice sounded strained, even to her own ears. "You can see how he has a black hat covering his hair, and the collar of his leather coat turned up and is wearing a black scarf, just like in the video outside the precinct. I can't even tell the color of his skin from this angle."

"Yeah, he's clearly trying to hide his identity."

She stared at the grainy photograph. The subway cameras weren't top of the line, but adequate for most things. Tayron Lee had a lean build, and she couldn't tell from the picture on the screen if that was him or not. She resumed the video.

The man dressed in black hesitated near the turnstile for several long moments, keeping his head down the entire time. When the train arrived, he made his move, crossing over toward her. His gloved hand came out of his pocket, and she could see the silver blade of the knife.

"Pause it there," Max said. "Zoom in on his face."

Tearing her gaze from the knife, she did as he requested, slowing the video frame by frame in an attempt to get the best view of his face.

The guy kept his head tipped down, almost as if he knew where the cameras were located. As she moved the video forward, she saw the moment his arm lashed out, the knife going into her red coat.

There was a second of nothing, then he jerked the knife out and turned away. Yet there still wasn't a good view of his face, even from the second camera angle.

She played the video until the guy was out of camera view. "Give me a moment to find the street video to pick up which direction he went."

She played with the video a bit more, bringing the street view up on a third screen. The guy headed left instead of to the right, and all they saw was his back as he ran away.

"Well, that was a bust."

Max's hands came up to lightly grasp her shoulders. "I'm sorry, Eden."

She felt ridiculously close to tears, which wasn't like her in the least. She forced confidence in her tone. "Sorry for what? I'll find him. There has to be a camera somewhere in the city that captured his face. He can't know where every camera on the street is located."

"If anyone can do it, you can." Max's hands tightened momentarily before dropping away. She instantly missed his warm touch. "We need to get to the staff meeting soon, but I want you to promise me you won't go anywhere alone."

She twisted around to look up at him. "Well, I can promise to try, but I can't stay here forever."

His blue gaze didn't waver. "Call me if you need to leave. In fact—" he glanced down at his watch "—why don't we plan to have lunch together? We'll head over to the 646 Diner. I'm in the mood for one of their cheeseburgers."

Her pulse skipped, but she knew better than to think of this as some sort of date. Max was only trying to lighten the mood after the horrible start to the day. "Sounds good. I'll see if anyone else is able to join us."

For a moment she thought she saw a flash of disappointment in his eyes, but it was gone so quickly she figured it was nothing more than her imagination. "The more the merrier."

Eden watched as Max headed out the door, willing her heart to return to its normal rhythm. First breakfast, and now lunch.

She gave herself a mental shake. Completely ridiculous to be so excited about having lunch at the 646 Diner. It was a cop hangout, so even more of a reason it wasn't a date.

Eden turned back to her computer screens to continue searching the video. It felt a bit like searching through a sandy beach for a diamond, but she was determined to get a picture of the assailant.

The stabbing and the snow-globe bomb were more than enough. She needed this guy behind bars before Christmas.

After leaving Eden, Max went straight to Sergeant Gavin Sutherland's office. He knocked, then strode in without waiting for a response.

"I want Eden protected."

"And you couldn't wait for the staff meeting to bring this up?" Gavin had been promoted from the NYC K-9 Command Unit in Queens about a year ago, when they'd created this unit in Brooklyn. Max found Gavin to be a good boss and was thankful for the opportunity to work with him.

Max knew he was overstepping his bounds but pushed forward. "We just watched the video. The guy who left the snow-globe bomb is the same one that stabbed her at the subway."

"And you think the perp is this Tayron Lee character?"

"Possibly. I checked his background. He has a couple of disorderly conduct tickets, last one about a year ago, but no arrests." He hesitated, then added, "I'm concerned about gang connections. Tayron likes to be called *Tiger* and he calls Eden's brother, Ricky, *Rat*. Some gangs use nicknames to hide their true identities."

Gavin scowled. "I don't like the thought of Eden's brother being involved."

"I know." He'd been torn about mentioning it, but his concern about Eden's safety overruled the possible conflict of interest. Another reason he hadn't waited for the staff meeting. "They lost their father when Eden was eighteen, her older brother, twenty-one. Ricky dropped out of college, but Eden excelled, skipping a grade and graduating early. As I'm sure you know,

NYPD recruited her from college for her technical skills. She feels working here is a way to honor her father's memory. She would never do anything to compromise her job here."

"Her dad was a great cop, served the city well for twenty years." Gavin tapped his pen on the surface of his desk. "Kent Chang was a straight shooter, and we know there isn't anyone who can replace Eden on our team. But we could ask Danielle Kowalski, the technical specialist from the Queens unit, to pick up the investigation now that we know Eden is a target."

Removing Eden from the investigation would be best since it was difficult to remain objective when family was involved, but Max hesitated. "I don't think that will go over well with her. I mean, it's her life on the line and she's the best one to view and enhance any video we find on this guy. As a witness, she would be the one to identify him. Besides, she already suspects Tayron Lee. No reason to think her view will be clouded by the fact the guy is her brother's friend. In fact, she seemed happy to have him questioned."

Gavin didn't speak for a long moment as if weighing the pros and cons. "Okay, she can work the case for now. But if we find out Tayron is involved, then we shift the work to Danielle in the Queens unit, okay?"

"Sounds good." Max tried not to let his relief show. "In the meantime, we need to keep Eden protected."

"You've been doing a good job of that so far. May as well keep on it." Gavin glanced at his watch. "Let's head over to the conference room. The others will be joining us shortly."

"Okay." He hadn't really expected Gavin to keep him on the job of protection detail yet couldn't deny the overwhelming sense of relief. The idea of Eden being in danger was bad enough. Putting her safety in someone else's hands would have been even more difficult. The Brooklyn K-9 Unit had a slew of very talented officers and detectives. They were all more than capable to protect Eden.

But this one was personal. After secretly

admiring her for so long, he didn't like knowing she was in danger.

When the entire team was assembled, Gavin filled everyone in on the recent events. He finished the meeting by explaining that Max would be on protection duty for Eden. He felt Eden's gaze on him but didn't dare meet her eyes.

"Sarge?" He waited until Gavin glanced at him. "What about the subway patrols? I worked extra last night after we received word about a ring of subway robberies, but it was fairly quiet." Until the knife attack on Eden.

Gavin's gaze turned thoughtful. "Belle works the subway, too, and if we get another threat of some kind, we'll find someone else to watch over Eden."

Max nodded. "Thanks."

After the staff meeting, Max went over to the training center to get Sam. His partner was overjoyed to see him and eager to get to work.

He and Sam returned to the Bay Ridge Avenue subway station, retracing the perp's steps from the night before. He'd wanted to kick himself for going to the right last night in an attempt to grab the guy. At the time it had seemed the most logical direction, but he'd been wrong.

The attacker was smart enough to avoid taking the less likely route to escape. Heading left kept him in view of the subway entrance longer, rather than going to the right to slink around the corner. A calculated risk that had paid off.

Max paused outside the Bay Ridge Avenue subway station and looked down the street in the direction the perp had taken. There were several bodegas and shops, any of which could have been used as an escape route. If they were still open at ten thirty at night.

He took Sam down the street, making frequent stops along the way, taking note of which ones were open late. When he realized it was more than he'd anticipated, he called Eden. "Do me a favor and look at the video of your assailant leaving the subway station. Can you see if he might have ducked into one of the shops along the avenue?"

"I'm looking at that section of the video right now. It's not as easy to see him as I'd hoped. I'm trying to pick him up with another camera."

He could hear her fingers clicking on the keyboard. He continued walking, trying to figure out which way the guy may have gone.

"I have the next camera up but haven't seen him yet." Her tone was laced with frustration. "It's like he disappeared into thin air."

"He had to have gone through one of the stores to duck out the back." He swept his gaze over the area. "These places look decent, no indication they'd house a criminal."

"I'll keep looking and will let you know if I find him."

"Okay." He made the rounds at every business that was open the night before, asking about the guy dressed in black and requesting video footage. By the time he finished, he was cold and hungry. It wasn't quite time for lunch, but knowing Sam needed a break, too, he headed back to the precinct.

After placing Sam in one of the kennels, he made his way to Eden's workstation. "Find anything?"

She turned to glance at him, her expression weary. "Not yet. I don't understand it. He had to have gone somewhere."

"Yeah." Her spicy scent was difficult to ignore as he joined her at the workstation. "I questioned ten business owners and looked at their video feeds but haven't found any sign of him."

"No one disappears in New York City." She let out a frustrated sigh. "I really thought I'd have something by now."

"Hey, it's early. We'll get him." He tried to sound reassuring but had a bad feeling that whoever this guy was, he was knowledgeable enough to have planned an escape route that kept him off the radar. "How well does Tayron know the area?"

She looked thoughtful. "I'm not sure where he grew up, but he went to the same high school Ricky and I attended. They both went to college, too, but never finished." Her voice held a note of bitterness.

"And you grew up in Dyker Heights?"

She nodded. "Why?"

"I'm just trying to get a feel for the guy." He cleared his throat. "According to Clayborn, there's still no sign of Tayron."

Eden's lips tightened and she picked up her cell phone. "Ricky, it's me. I need you to call me, okay? It's important."

"Do you think he'll return your call?"

"I don't know." Her dark gaze was troubled. "Lately, he hasn't been returning my calls as quickly as he used to."

Max hesitated. "Could he be doing something illegal?"

She opened her mouth as if to instinctively deny the allegation, then hesitated. She nodded. "Yes, unfortunately. Ricky took my dad's death hard, and I believe Tayron took advantage of that, steering him down a dangerous path. Maybe he wants to get rid of me, because I'm trying to pull Ricky back from whatever he's mixed up in."

He could tell the idea distressed her and

had to hold himself back from taking her into his arms. "Hey, I know it's early, but why don't we head over to the diner? Do you know if anyone else is able to join us?"

A dark flush stained her cheeks and he wondered why she felt embarrassed. "Penny said she's waiting for Tyler to get back to her, and if he does, they might be able to make it. Unfortunately, the rest of the team are spread out across the borough."

"Hey, it's not a big deal." He was secretly pleased to have her to himself for a while. "Looks like you could use a break, no need to wait for Penny and Tyler."

"A break would be good." She rubbed her eyes, then shut down her computer. "Are you bringing Sam with us?"

He was pleased she seemed to care about his K-9 partner. "Might as well since the guy who owns the diner allows our K-9s inside."

"Okay." She turned toward the door and reached for her coat. He took it from her and held it up so she could slip her arms into the sleeves. "Thanks." Her voice was so quiet he had to lean forward to hear.

"You're welcome." Once they reached the first floor, he briefly left to fetch Sam from the kennels while Eden promised to wait for him at the front desk.

He hurried back with Sam just as Penny hung up the phone, jotting down some notes. "Hey, Penny, we're heading over to the 646 for lunch."

Penny nodded. "I just spoke to Tyler. He's running late. No need to wait. You two should eat while you can."

"Okay." Eden turned to face him. "All set?"

"Absolutely." He couldn't help but grin. "After you."

She led the way outside. The walk to the diner didn't take long. The place was packed as usual, but when two spots opened up at the counter on the corner, allowing a place for Sam to lie down comfortably and out of the way, he quickly snagged them.

"Do you need a menu?" He glanced at her. "I have it memorized, but then again, I eat here far more than I should."

She smiled and he found himself captivated by the light shining from her dark eyes.

The server came to take their order. "I'll have coffee and a cheeseburger loaded with the works."

"I'll have green tea, please, and a Cobb salad." She glanced at him. "Maybe you'll share your fries?"

"Absolutely." He chuckled and it occurred to him that it had been a long time since he'd enjoyed spending time with a woman. Playing pickup basketball with the guys was fine, but this was different.

Nicer.

"Hey, there's peanut-butter-cup ice cream for dessert." He wiggled his eyebrows. "What do you think?"

She smiled and shook her head. "Not for me—I have a severe peanut allergy."

He hadn't known about that. "Okay, no peanuts. But if I remember correctly, they have peppermint cheesecake, too."

She held up a hand in protest. "The Cobb salad and stealing a few of your fries is enough for me, thanks."

"We could share one." He liked teasing her. "After all, Christmas is less than a week away. Why not celebrate?"

She shook her head, but her smile was warm. "What are your plans for the holiday?"

Her innocent question caught him off guard. "I offered to work. I figured as one of the single guys, I should let the married and engaged couples have the day off."

"I offered to work, too." She wrinkled her nose and glanced away. "Normally I try to spend time with Ricky, but I doubt that will happen this year."

"Christmas is about families, isn't it?" He looked at the way her slender fingers cupped her steaming tea. "I lost my fiancée just over a year ago, and I'm dreading the upcoming holiday."

"Oh, Max. I'm sorry to hear that." She rested her hand on his arm.

"Thanks." Telling her about Jessica wasn't something he'd planned, but he felt better having told her. It wasn't that he cared if others knew, but he preferred not to talk about it.

His burger and her salad were set before them. Eden bowed her head and silently prayed, then glanced over at him with a mischievous grin. She leaned over and scooped several french fries off his plate. "Yum."

He chuckled again. "You're welcome." He remembered how Jessica used to pray before meals, too. He'd gone to church with her, but since her death, had found himself unable to attend services.

He took a bite of his burger. For several minutes they enjoyed their respective meals when suddenly Eden's hand clamped tightly down on his arm.

"What is it?" He glanced at her. She had one hand at her throat, her eyes wide with fear. Panic seized him. "Eden? What do you need?"

"Can't breathe..." She pulled something out of her pocket, but it fell to the floor.

He jumped off the stool and grabbed what he now realized was an epinephrine injector. All cops were trained in the basics of first aid, including administering Narcan and epinephrine, but his hands shook as he took the device in his hand.

A strangled sound came from her throat and he knew there wasn't a moment to waste. He caught the gaze of the woman behind the counter. "Call 911!" He jammed the syringe through her slacks into the muscle of her thigh and gave the injection.

The medication worked, and after a moment she was able to speak, her voice still hoarse. "Peanut oil."

"Where?" He glanced around in confusion.

She gestured to her salad. What? He didn't understand. The Cobb salad didn't come with peanuts in any way, shape or form. He leaned forward to sniff at her salad and caught the faint scent of peanut oil.

He scowled, raking his gaze over the crowded diner. This wasn't an accident. This had been done on purpose. By someone who knew exactly how Eden would be affected.

FOUR

Eden took a couple of deep breaths using the oxygen mask the paramedics provided. Her thigh ached where she'd gotten the epinephrine injection, but she ignored the pain. Max's quick thinking, the way he'd instantly understood what needed to be done, had saved her life.

God had been watching out for her.

"Your heart rate is still very fast," the paramedic with an ID tag indicating his name was Weston said. "We need to get you to the closest emergency department to be evaluated."

She moved the face mask to the side so she could speak. "My pulse is up because epinephrine is a stimulant. As soon as the medication wears off, I'll be fine."

Weston scowled. "Maybe, but we still need to take you in."

She shook her head, took one last deep breath of oxygen, then handed him the mask. "I've been through this before, and promise I'll be fine."

"You'll have to sign a waiver," the second paramedic said. She couldn't see his name. "And make sure you read the risks of not going in to be evaluated, including the possibility of death."

"I know the risks, but as I said, this isn't my first allergic reaction. And I only took a small bite of my salad." She took the clipboard from the paramedic's hand and signed the waiver. "Thanks for coming."

The two paramedics looked at each other, shrugged and packed their equipment up onto the gurney.

Eden sat next to Sam, watching as Max spoke to one diner customer after another in an attempt to understand what had happened. There were several cops there from other precincts who joined in. From what she could overhear, the answers weren't helpful.

No one saw anyone doing anything near her salad.

Joe Best, former cop and owner of the diner, limped over, his brow deeply furrowed with concern. They all knew that Joe had been seriously injured on the job, forcing him into early retirement. He opened the diner after. "Officer Santelli? I just heard what happened."

Max shook hands with Joe, then gestured to her. "You remember our technical specialist, Eden Chang. Someone doused her salad with peanut oil in a deliberate attempt to harm her. She's allergic. I'd like to interview your kitchen crew."

"Of course." Joe stepped back. "You know I'll always cooperate with the police."

Eden slid off her stool, her legs still a bit shaky. Max told Sam to stay. She followed Max into the kitchen, unwilling to be left out of the investigation.

The interviews didn't take long. Each of the kitchen staff adamantly denied having anything to do with the peanut oil incident and based on the fact that Joe was a former cop and would vet his employees carefully, she was inclined to believe them. After taking each staff member's name and phone number, Max searched the kitchen for the source of the peanut oil.

There was nothing to find. No bottle of peanut oil lying around that might be used by mistake. Even the peanut-butter-cup ice cream came prepackaged and was not likely to be a cross-contaminant.

"We need to get back to the precinct," Eden said as Max tucked his notebook into the pocket of his uniform. "We might find something on the cameras surrounding the building."

Max nodded. "Okay, fine. But you'd better be prepared to answer to Gavin about refusing to go to the ER."

"I'm fine. Not sure why you don't believe me." Eden didn't appreciate his lack of support. She wasn't an idiot. She'd know if she needed additional medical attention.

Thankfully, she'd only taken one bite of her salad, or her reaction could have been much worse.

"Hold on." Joe came out with two to-go boxes. "Replacement meals on the house.

I made them myself. And I'm putting up a five grand reward for anyone who helps solve this crime."

Max lifted a brow. "That's a lot of money."

Joe scowled. "I take this attack on Eden personally. I won't tolerate this type of criminal behavior in my diner."

"Once a cop, always a cop." Max smiled.

"Thank you, Joe." Eden took the boxes from him.

Max put Sam on his leash and together they walked outside. Once they were alone, he glanced at her. "I've never been so scared."

His frank admission surprised her. "You did great. I appreciate you saving my life."

He shook his head. "They teach us to do this kind of thing but the reality is far different."

"I know." She patted his arm. "But you were amazing."

Max fell silent as they made their way back to the precinct. He and Sam accompanied her to her workstation, where she quickly pulled up the video from the streetlights closest to the diner.

"Are you hungry?" He glanced at her. "You only ate a couple of fries."

"Not really," she answered absently, her gaze never wavering from the screen.

Max set her salad on the edge of her workstation. She chose to eat yogurt from the mini-fridge instead, while watching the video feed.

By the time she'd finished, she still didn't have any inclination of who had tried to harm her. She sat back in her seat and sighed.

"I just don't get it. Where could he have gone?"

"He?" Max had eaten his cheeseburger while watching the video, too. "You think Tayron Lee did this?"

"He knows about my peanut allergy."

"Don't your friends know, too?"

She glanced at him. "Yes. But Tayron is the only person I can think of with an ax to grind. Not just because I repeatedly refused to go out with him, but because I attempt to keep my brother away from him."

He nodded. "Who knows you've moved to Sunset Park?"

She thought about this. "My roommate, of course, but she's in Colorado. My Geek Quad friends helped me move in. I honestly haven't told Ricky about our new place, because I didn't want Tayron to know."

"The Geek Quad helped you move."

"Yes, so what if they did?"

"I just think that whoever did this is someone very close to you." He gestured to the screen where there was no one remotely suspicious-looking going in or out of the diner. "You recently moved, haven't told Tayron Lee or your brother where you live, and this guy definitely knows your address since he left bomb residue on your apartment doorknob and seems to know where every camera in the area is located."

She frowned, not liking where this was going.

"It makes me wonder if Tayron Lee is sophisticated enough to elude the authorities like this. Whereas your Geek Quad friends are very smart, tech savvy enough to hack into the cameras, know where you live and know about your allergy."

"I can't believe it." She couldn't imagine any of her friends being involved. But working around cops, she understood it was just as important to clear people from suspicion. Darnell Hicks and Bryon Avery were both average height and weight. Darnell had dark hair, and Bryon's hair was light brown. Tom Gellner was taller than the other two and wore his red hair short. They were computer nerds, like her. She couldn't imagine they were involved. "I've known Darnell, Tom and Bryon for nearly a decade. I get they have amazing tech skills, but they have no reason to hurt me. Go ahead and check them out. I'm sure you'll be able to clear all three of them, especially since they all work for the government."

"Working for the government doesn't mean incapable of committing a crime."

Max's light blue eyes bored into hers. He was right, of course. But she still didn't want to believe it. "I know."

"When is the last time you've seen these guys?"

"Just last week. We get together often, mostly for gaming competitions, sometimes in person, sometimes online, but generally every two weeks or so to keep up our tech skills."

"Gaming, huh?" He looked surprised by that, but she refused to be embarrassed. Maybe she wasn't the most athletically inclined person in Brooklyn, but she was smart. And gaming helped hone her tech skills. "You physically met in person just a week ago?"

"Yes." She waved a hand. "We often meet at a place called The Center. It's a gaming store that caters to serious gamers."

He frowned. "And what, the store has a large room where gamers can get together?"

"Exactly." She shrugged. "It's neutral territory and Chris, the owner, sets up tournaments and stuff."

"I see." When Max rose to his feet, Sam did, too. "I need to do some digging into their backgrounds. Will you please stay here and wait for me? I don't want you to go anywhere alone."

With a grimace, she reluctantly nodded. "I'll wait."

"Thanks."

She watched as Max and Sam left, then

thought back to the last time she'd gotten together with the Geek Quad. That day, she hadn't noticed anything out of the ordinary. They'd all been intense about the game, eager to knock each other out of the competition. They played to win, and frankly, she'd always appreciated how the guys treated her like one of the guys, and not a girl they might be interested in.

It just didn't make sense that one of them would turn on her to the point of trying to hurt her.

To nearly kill her.

She forced herself to focus on the video. The real culprit had to be Tayron Lee. It was entirely possible she and Max weren't giving him enough credit.

Tayron and Ricky had attended three years of college. They weren't stupid. Misguided, yes, but not stupid.

She felt certain Tayron Lee was involved. And that once he was found and questioned, the danger would be over.

Leaving her to go back to her dull life. One in which Max wasn't with her every minute of every day.

* * *

Max kenneled Sam, then went to his cubicle. He wrote up the report about what had transpired at the 646 Diner. Once that was finished and sent off to Gavin, he began investigating the three members of Eden's Geek Quad. It pained him to think someone she called a friend would do something like this, but he wasn't about to overlook any possibility.

Unfortunately, there wasn't much to find. Each of them had squeaky-clean backgrounds. Nothing remotely close to indicating a predilection for criminal behavior. He made a note to ask Eden about other techy friends she might have, other than the Geek Quad.

"Max?"

He glanced up as Gavin Sutherland approached his cubicle. "Yeah, Sarge?"

"My office," Gavin said, leaving Max to follow.

Gavin waved him toward the chair, but he didn't move. "I prefer to stand when getting chewed out."

Gavin flashed a crooked smile. "Who

said I was upset? I just finished reviewing your report on Eden's allergic reaction. Are you sure this was done intentionally?"

"Absolutely certain." He didn't hesitate. "As I indicated in my report, there was no peanut oil in the kitchen. I don't see how this could be anything but a targeted attack on Eden."

Gavin nodded slowly. "Still nothing on Tayron Lee?"

"No, and that's a problem. It's seems as if the guy is hiding from the police. He didn't show up for his scheduled shift at the warehouse today and hasn't returned to the apartment he shares with Eden's brother, Ricky."

"No sign of Eden's brother, either?"

"No." Max knew it was likely the two guys were hiding out together. Because of the attack on Eden? Or something else?

Unfortunately, anything was possible.

"I don't like it," Gavin said with a deep frown. "It's odd that someone would have known Eden was going to the diner for lunch today."

Max straightened in his seat as Gavin's

point hit home. "You're right. We didn't make lunch plans ahead of time, only just decided to head over there this morning."

"Which means the perp is following her or watching from someplace nearby."

"Yeah. And that would explain how the perp knew when she'd walked away from the precinct last night. The video shows the guy in black leaving the bomb for her, then catching up to her at the subway." He sprang to his feet. "I need to check out all the businesses nearby, see if I can pinpoint a potential stakeout location."

"Let me know what you find."

"Will do." Max returned to his cubicle.

There were times police work was tedious and pulling up information on the adjacent properties to the precinct was exactly that. But he managed to identify two distinct possibilities. Each were brown brick buildings, one had a real-estate business and fast-food restaurant on the main level with apartments up above, and the other had a coffee shop and drugstore on the main level, also with apartments above.

The fact that there were so many apartments was depressing. It offered far too many possibilities. But he was leaning toward the fast-food restaurant and drugstore as the likely source. They were public places where anyone could linger without drawing attention. And they were open until 11:00 p.m.

The coffee shop closed at nine o'clock, so he didn't think the perp had been there that first night, but certainly could be rotating the places he used to observe the precinct.

Armed with this new information, he rose, stretched and glanced around, surprised to note the time was well past five o'clock and many of the cubicles around him were empty.

He went down to get Sam out of his kennel. After taking his partner outside and working with him for a few minutes, he headed up to Eden's workspace.

She was leaning on her desk, rubbing her temples.

"Are you okay?"

She startled and turned to face him. "Yes. Just battling a headache, a common side effect of epinephrine."

He nodded. "Sorry to hear that. Find anything?"

"Not much." She let out a sigh and began to scroll through her various video feeds. "I was able to find an image of a man in black leaving the restaurant from the back door roughly six minutes before my salad was set in front of me. The quality of the camera is lousy, though. I've been playing with it to sharpen the image but without much success."

He leaned over to see the figure she indicated. The camera was awful, and the guy on the screen kept his head down. "Doubt we'd get a good look at his face, even if the image were clear."

"I know. And he goes two blocks, then disappears from view. I haven't been able to pick him up, yet."

"I'll question the staff again. Someone must have seen him." He lightly rested his hand on her slim shoulder. "Hang in there. We have another potential lead. What if this guy has been watching you come and go from either the fast-food restaurant, coffee shop or drugstore? It's clear he's been following you."

Eden's eyes widened as the realization sank deep. Within seconds she was pulling up the closest camera footage.

They watched in silence as various people went in and out of the fast-food restaurant next to the K-9 Unit. Then a familiar man dressed in black arrived. She hit the pause button. "There! That's him."

"Yeah, it sure is." He wrapped his arm around her shoulders and gave her a quick hug. "Now that we know he's watching the front of the precinct, we'll use the rear exit."

"Yeah, but I want to record him following me first." She played with the controls, and then ran snippets of the video feed, saving them to another location. It wasn't easy to concentrate with her warm, spicy scent teasing his senses.

"I have him leaving the fast-food restaurant just ten seconds after we walked toward the 646," Eden said with satisfaction. "I can track him following me to the diner and to the subway the evening before. This will be key evidence when we finally get him."

"Trust me, we won't stop until we have him behind bars." Max spoke with confidence.

"I know." She smiled when Sam pressed his nose against her.

The phone on her workstation rang, and she hit the speaker button so Max could hear, too. "Chang," she answered.

"Eden, it's Darcy from the crime lab. I just wanted to let you know we did not find any fingerprints on the snow globe or the package."

"Darcy, this is Max Santelli. What about the bomb itself?"

"We're still working on that with the bomb squad. They believe the device was armed to detonate from a remote trigger."

There was a long moment of silence before Eden spoke. "Thanks, Darcy." She disconnected from the call, and her shoulders slumped with dejection. "Back to grainy images of our perp."

"We'll get him. But right now, you need to take a break."

She nodded, pushed back her chair and stood. When she swayed a bit, he lightly grasped her shoulders. "Whoa, are you all right?"

"Fine." Her voice was soft, breathless.

"Eden." He drew her slowly into a warm embrace. "I'm here for you."

"I appreciate that, Max." Rather than pulling away, she tipped her head back to gaze up at him. For long moments neither of them spoke, the air shimmering with awareness.

The urge to kiss her was incredibly strong. He forced himself to release her, his mind whirling.

The close call struck deep. In the year since losing Jessica, he'd never wanted to kiss a woman the way he longed to with Eden.

And he had no idea what to do about that.

FIVE

Eden leaned against her workstation, hoping her innate reaction to being held in Max's embrace wasn't written in bold letters on her forehead.

They'd almost kissed. *Almost* being the operative word.

She licked suddenly dry lips. Why on earth was she so keenly aware of Max on a personal level? They were colleagues, forced to work together because she'd become a target.

She needed to keep her head in the game. To stay focused.

Kissing Max Santelli was not allowed.

"How long are you planning to work tonight?"

She glanced up at Max, his gaze difficult to read. "Probably not much longer. I'm worried this nagging headache will cause me to miss something." She didn't add the issue of her blurry vision. It wasn't related to the shot of epinephrine, but from staring at the computer screen.

"Yeah, I'm feeling a little fried myself. Are you interested in stopping to pick up something to eat on the way home? Pizza sounds good right about now."

Home? Her dry mouth intensified. Logic dictated Max was only trying to protect her, but did he really need to sleep on her sofa for a second night?

And why did she secretly want him to?

"If you don't like pizza, we can get something else," Max said, misinterpreting her silence.

"Pizza is great. But you don't need to stay overnight again. I'm sure I'll be safe enough."

His blue eyes bored into hers for a long moment before he shrugged. "That's fine, but since we both have to eat, let's pick up something once we get to Sunset Park."

"Sounds good." Eden packed her personal laptop in its case and slung the strap crossways across her torso before pulling her coat on.

"Why do you haul your personal laptop back and forth each day?" Max asked.

She flushed and ducked her chin. "Normally I go online over my lunch break, you know, to check in with the Geek Quad, that kind of thing. I also practice some technical things."

He lifted a brow as he clipped a leash to Sam's collar. "Like hacking?"

"Yes, exactly like that. We don't just do gaming. We create security systems for each other and practice hacking through them. I figure it's better for me to do that on my own time and on my own equipment, just in case something goes wrong."

"Makes sense. Come, Sam," Max said, giving his K-9 partner a hand signal. The Rottweiler moved to his side.

Eden decided not to mention the fact that having lunch at the 646 with Max was the closest thing she'd had to a date since college. And it hadn't been a date, more of a coworker bonding experience. Especially if you consider how Max was forced to jab her with epinephrine to save her life.

He led the way down to the main level, then out through the exit located in the back side of the building. Hunching her shoulders against the blast of cold air, she accompanied him on a circuitous route to the subway. Sam's head swiveled around, his nose in the air as he took in the various scents surrounding them.

"He's a good K-9 cop," she said, as they approached a different subway entrance than the one she'd used the night before. "I'm impressed with his ability to find bombs."

"The best partner I've ever had," Max agreed, bending over to give Sam a quick rub. "Being assigned to the subway is sometimes more mundane work than I'd like, but still important. Especially when we get bomb threats."

"I can only imagine." She was struck by the fact that Max, like her father, was the one who would run toward danger when most everyone else ran in the opposite direction.

Her father had died of cancer, but she'd heard about the occasional close call he'd experienced in the line of duty. The way Max was constantly on alert, sweeping his gaze over the area in an attempt to find the man dressed in black, was proof that he'd do anything necessary to keep her and other innocent victims safe.

Just like her father.

It was honorable work and she was glad to be a part of it. But being in danger gave her a different perspective. The danger her father had faced and the cops she worked with confronted every day was very real. God obviously had a plan and it wasn't her place to question Him. But it wouldn't hurt to protect her heart from becoming too vulnerable.

"I know Sal's is a favorite pizzeria, but there's another place by the name of Rodolfo's Pizzeria, located a few blocks from my building." Max glanced at her. "Do you know it?"

"Yes, I've stopped there a couple of times. Works for me."

"Great." The subway doors opened, and

passengers streamed out, giving Sam a wide berth. The K-9's vest labeled him as a K-9 cop, but he was a big and intimidating animal.

It was standing room only at this hour and she tried not to allow Max's sandalwood scent to distract her.

"Do you have other tech-savvy friends?"

She lifted a brow. "I had some people I was friendly with during college but haven't kept in touch over the past six years. Why?"

"Just curious. I still think that the way this guy stays out of camera range is suspicious." He was silent for a moment, then asked, "When are you planning another Geek Quad get-together?"

"Next week—Monday, I believe. It's more of a holiday party than a gaming session."

"You don't mind if I tag along?"

Max's question was spoken like a statement rather than a question. While she didn't think she was in danger from any of her friends, she could secretly admit that she didn't relish the thought of traveling across town alone. "I don't mind, but the guys will badger you with questions. Showing up together will also make them read more into our relationship than there is."

"I don't mind." Max's blue eyes clung to hers. She tightened her grip on the pole, feeling as if she might drown in their azure depths.

There was nothing she could say to that, so she left it alone.

They got off before their regular stop in order to pick up a pizza from Rodolfo's. As they stood in line at the counter, she realized Max had done this on purpose to throw off the perp. Taken them to a different subway station to catch the train and getting off at a different location than she normally used. All in the guise of getting pizza.

No point in complaining. Besides, she felt safe with Max and Sam at her side.

Max insisted on carrying the pizza as they walked the few blocks to her apartment. He chose a path that brought them up along the back of the building rather than the front.

She glanced fugitively over her shoulder as she used her key to open the main door.

Hopefully, if the guy in black was lurking around outside, he'd take off after seeing her with Max and Sam.

When she opened her apartment door, she heard Charlie meowing loudly. Distressed at how long she'd been gone coupled with showing up once again with Sam, no doubt.

"Poor kitty," she said, as Max placed the pizza box on the table. "He's not sure what to make of this."

"Something tells me that cat can hold his own." Max's wry tone made her smile.

The cat howled again and raced past them from a hiding spot behind the sofa.

Sam let out a series of sharp barks.

"Quiet," Max said sternly.

The baleful expression Sam sent over his shoulder to Max made her laugh for the first time in what seemed like forever. As if the K-9 understood exactly what was going on.

And wasn't at all happy about it.

They sat down to eat. She murmured a quick prayer before digging in. The pizza had cooled off during their short walk. Smelling the spicy tomato and pepperoni made her mouth water and her stomach growl with anticipation.

Max didn't say much as they devoured the pie. When his phone rang, he pulled it from his pocket and frowned at the number on the screen. "Sarge? What's up?"

She couldn't hear their boss's side of the conversation, but the icy look in Max's eyes was not reassuring.

"Okay, thanks. I'll let Eden know and head over there ASAP." He disconnected from the call and stood.

"Let me know what?"

Max's expression was grim. "There was a stabbing attack on the subway less than an hour ago. Victim is a Chinese-American female."

Chinese-American? Like her? "You think this is some sort of copycat attack?"

"I'm not sure what to think. Could be completely unrelated, but the coincidence of being stabbed with a knife is something we don't dare ignore."

A chill rippled down her back. "A knife? She was attacked by a man with a knife?"

"I'm afraid so. And the attack happened

a few minutes after the train left the Bay Ridge station." Max looked apologetic. "I have to go, but I want you to stay here with the door locked, okay?"

Her throat was so tight she couldn't speak. She nodded.

"Sam, Come." Max bent over to clip the K-9's leash to his collar. As they made their way to her door, she forced herself to follow.

Max opened the apartment door, then glanced at her. "I'll call you when I find out something more."

"Okay." She forced the word past her constricted vocal cords. When he and Sam headed out, she closed the door and shot the dead bolt home.

Another knife attack on the subway, with a victim of Chinese heritage.

She leaned weakly against the door. A coincidence or a pattern of deviant behavior?

Was it possible the attack with the knife wasn't related to the snow-globe bomb? She couldn't imagine one person trying to harm her, much less two of them.

Unfortunately, this nightmare was all too real.

* * *

Leaving Eden alone was the most difficult thing he'd done since losing Jessica. Jogging to the subway station, he pulled out his phone to call Gavin.

He'd been tempted to leave Sam with her as added protection, but knew that wouldn't fly with his boss. So he decided to request the next best thing. "Someone needs to watch Eden while I'm gone."

"I've already asked Henry Roarke and his K-9, Cody, to swing by her apartment." Gavin paused, then asked, "What's your ETA?"

"I'm getting a rideshare now, should arrive at the Bay Ridge stop in ten to fifteen minutes." Max relaxed a bit, knowing Henry and Cody, his bomb-sniffing beagle, were on their way. He trusted Henry to keep watch over Eden.

Henry Roarke was engaged to Olivia Vance, his former nemesis from the Office of Internal Affairs. Some of the single guys on the force had mentioned how pretty Eden was and he wondered if she was interested in any of them. Not that it should matter to him one way or the other. Eden could date whomever she wanted. He wasn't interested in a relationship.

Despite the fact that he'd almost kissed her senseless.

When he arrived at the Bay Ridge stop, he took the stairs up to street level two at a time. The victim was seated in the back of a police cruiser, her long dark hair partially covering her face.

He stopped short when he saw that the woman wore a red winter coat. It wasn't exactly like Eden's, but similar.

Close enough to have confused the attacker into believing the woman was Eden?

Was this attack a case of mistaken identity?

"Max." Gavin nodded at him with a grim expression. "You can see why I needed you here."

"Yeah." Most cops didn't believe in coincidences and he was one of them. He kept his voice low so the victim couldn't overhear. "The question is, did he attack her by mistake? Or on purpose because Eden thwarted his attempt to follow her?"

"Neither scenario is a good one," Gavin admitted. "Her name is Patti Wang, and she works in real estate. See what you can glean from her. She isn't hurt badly. The EMTs bandaged the shallow wound on her arm, but she's shaken up by the attack."

Who wouldn't be? Max nodded, then opened the door of the cruiser and crouched down so he wouldn't look so intimidating. "Sam, Sit."

His K-9 partner sat.

"Hi, Ms. Wang, I'm Officer Max Santelli, and this is my partner, Sam." He smiled in a way that he hoped was reassuring. "I know you've already spoken to the officers who came to your rescue, but would you please tell me what happened?"

Patti sniffed and rubbed at her nose. Her dark eyes were red from crying. "I was leaving the office where my friend works, you know the one across the street from the police station?"

The tiny hairs on the back of his neck rose in alarm. It was one of the businesses that he thought their assailant might be using as a watch point. "I'm familiar with the place. You don't work there?"

"No, but my friend Tabitha does. We were supposed to meet to take the subway together, but she got tied up in a delayed closing so I decided to head home." She twisted her fingers in her lap. "I didn't notice anyone behind me, but when I got down to the subway station, I felt someone come up behind me. When I turned, I saw the knife and tried to jerk away but the tip caught me along my upper arm. I screamed and the guy ran off."

The tear in her coat was long and deep, enough to have cut her skin through her clothing. Her story was eerily similar to what had happened to Eden. "Did you recognize him?"

"No." Patti sniffed again. "Why didn't anyone chase after him? Why did they let him get away?"

He gently changed the subject. "Do you have any enemies that might be carrying a grudge against you? Anyone at all that you think is capable of doing something like this?"

Patti hesitated. "To be honest, I thought the attacker might have been my ex-boyfriend."

An ex-boyfriend? Maybe this was a coincidence, after all. Max relaxed and dug his notebook from his breast pocket. "What's his name? I'd like to check up on that possibility, see if the guy has an alibi or not."

She blew out a breath. "His name is Ricky Chang."

Eden's brother? "How long have you known Ricky?"

"I met him about a year ago at one of the clubs. He seemed like a nice guy and all, but I didn't like his friend."

The hairs on his neck were standing straight upright. "Tayron Lee? Otherwise known as Tiger?"

Her eyes widened. "Yes. How did you know?"

He couldn't believe this woman dated Eden's brother. "Why did you two break up?"

She wrinkled her nose. "He got all possessive about me, saying I belonged to him and other nonsense. I think Tayron was egging him on."

"When's the last time you saw Ricky or Tayron?"

"Probably four months ago, maybe longer. I don't go to the clubs anymore because I'm focused on my career." She frowned. "You think Ricky had something to do with this?"

Ricky or Tayron or someone trying to divert attention away from himself and onto the most likely suspects.

Too bad Max had no idea which theory was the right one.

Before he could move away, his phone rang. He glanced down, recognizing Henry Roarke's number. Eden? He gripped the phone. "What's wrong?"

"Just as I was approaching Eden's building, I saw a guy dressed in black walking toward it. Cody and I gave chase, but he managed to get away."

"Eden's all right?"

"I texted her and she's fine. I'm heading back to stand guard outside her door now."

"Thanks." Max disconnected from the

call. Apparently, this attack on Patti Wang was nothing more than a diversionary tactic. Eden was still the prime target.

SIX

Unable to sit still, Eden paced the interior of her apartment. Charlie had finally crawled out from under her bed to eat his food. He was daintily licking his paws when her buzzer sounded.

She startled so bad she had to take a deep breath to calm herself as she crossed the room to the intercom. "Yes?"

"Eden? It's Max. Would you please let me in?"

"Of course." She hit the button that disengaged the lock, then hovered near her door until she heard the sound of footsteps approaching. After peering through the peephole to be sure Max and Sam were the ones out there, she shifted the dead bolt and opened the door. She tried to smile. "Hey."

His ominous expression had her stomach knotting with tension. "We need to talk."

She stepped back to give them room to enter, then closed and relocked the door behind him. Charlie let out a high-pitched meow and sprinted toward the sanctity of her bedroom. This time Sam didn't bark, but stood on alert, his nose quivering. The dog was growing accustomed to Charlie's presence.

Too bad she couldn't say the same about the cat.

"Good boy," Max praised, reaching down to rub his partner's silky coat. He shucked off his outer gear, then gestured toward the kitchen table.

She licked her dry lips and dropped weakly into the nearest chair. "I-is she hurt bad? She—didn't die, did she?"

"No, she's fine. The knife wound wasn't very deep. It was a shallow laceration, less than three inches long." Max's voice was calm and soothing. "Do you know Patti Wang?"

She frowned. "No, why? Should I?"

Max hesitated, then shrugged. "She apparently dated your brother. Ricky never introduced you?"

She thought back to the last few encounters she'd had with her brother, before shaking her head. "No, but I'm not surprised. He's been distancing himself from me lately. Hasn't returned my phone calls since I moved. I didn't know he had a girlfriend. How long has she been seeing him?"

"Several weeks, but she says she hasn't seen him for the past four months. Partially because she didn't like Tayron Lee."

She blew out a heavy sigh. "I don't know why my brother continues to hang out with him. He's not Tiger, but Trouble with a capital *T*."

Max studied her for a long moment. "She was followed to the subway from the real-estate office located across the street from the precinct. It's where her friend works."

The knot in her stomach tightened. "That's a strange coincidence."

"She looks a lot like you, Eden. But I don't think this is a case of mistaken identity." His gaze was full of concern. "Henry and his K-9, Cody, saw a man dressed in black heading toward this building. They scared him off, but I think it's clear the attack on her was a diversionary tactic."

A hard lump formed in the back of her throat. The thought that anyone would target an innocent person because of her was horrifying. "I—don't know what to say."

He reached over to cradle her hand in his. "This isn't your fault. But I think the attack on Patti was done to deliberately throw suspicion onto Tayron Lee, as if to make him look like a guy who attacks women."

Her mind whirled. "You think Tayron might be innocent? Who would know he was a suspect in the first place? Or know about my peanut allergy? And the fact that I collect snow globes?"

He shook his head. "I don't know. I keep coming back to your Geek Quad friends—they know where you live. They know how and when to divert their faces around cameras in the area."

"But why? There's no reason for my friends to hurt me."

He offered a wan smile. "I know, but I can't afford to ignore the tech angle related to the cameras. No common criminal is that good. We need to investigate all possibilities." He tightened his grip on her hand. "I'm not leaving you here alone tonight."

She swallowed hard, then nodded as a wave of relief washed over her. "Thank you. I appreciate that. Frankly, I was a nervous wreck the entire time you and Sam were gone, even knowing Henry was outside with Cody to alert."

Max's blue gaze clung to hers. "Trust me, Eden. None of us are going to let anything happen to you."

The idea that Max had cared enough to arrange for someone to watch over her was overwhelming and humbling. "Thank you."

He released her hand and turned toward his K-9. "I'll sleep on the sofa again."

She nodded and stood. "I'll get the things you used yesterday."

Eden stretched a sheet over the sofa, then set down the blanket and pillow. She stood for a moment, thinking about the limited amount of food in her fridge. "I should have stopped at the grocery store on the way home."

"Don't worry, we'll be fine." Max crossed over. "I might even give your green tea a try."

That made her smile. "It's better for you than coffee."

For the second time that day, awareness filled the air between them. He drew her into his arms for a hug, but then released her. "Good night, Eden."

"Good night." She had to force herself to turn and walk away.

She logged into her laptop computer, grimacing when she saw there was another email from the Federal recruiter who'd contacted her two weeks ago. He was once again asking for a meeting to discuss the various job opportunities they had for her.

She closed the laptop without replying. While it was tempting to respond to the guy, she knew deep down she really didn't want to leave the Brooklyn K-9 Unit.

Especially not after the way she'd grown closer to Max.

Max didn't sleep well. Eden's sofa was comfortable enough, and the Christmas lights on the tree were soothing, but the different twists in the case ricocheted through his brain.

The more he thought about it, the more he believed the attack on Patti Lee had been a diversion tactic. For one thing, the laceration on her arm wasn't very deep. Not to mention, her former relationship with Ricky Chang was far too much of a coincidence. And Henry and Cody had seen a guy in black approaching Eden's building.

Would Tayron Lee be so crazy as to attack his buddy's former girlfriend as a lame attempt to throw suspicion off him attacking Eden? Somehow, he couldn't see it.

Would one of her Geek Quad friends do something like that? Maybe, especially if they knew about Ricky and Tayron's friendship. But how would they know about Ricky's girlfriend when Eden hadn't even known about her?

What was the motive for all of this? Why would one of her friends come after her? And if not one of her close friends, then who?

He had far too many questions without answers.

Rolling off the sofa, he stretched and reached for his utility belt and weapon. Sam lifted his head, then lumbered to his feet. Sam headed toward the door, waiting patiently for Max to pull on his jacket, grab Eden's keys and the leash.

Outside, he swept his gaze over the area, searching for anyone who might be watching Eden's building, but the area was very residential. There was no one nearby and there were no businesses across the street where someone could hang out. Reassured, he headed back inside with Sam.

Eden was up and dressed when he entered the kitchen. She had a carton of eggs on the counter and was busy making what appeared to be veggie omelets.

"You don't have to cook for me," he protested as he unhooked Sam's leash. He crossed over to wash his hands in the sink beside her. The entire scene felt very domestic.

"It's my turn," she said with a smile. "I have the tea kettle on, too."

He tried not to wince—after all, he'd promised to give her green tea a try.

But man, he would have given a lot for a cup of coffee.

"Any news?" Eden glanced at him over her shoulder.

"Not yet." He was hoping they'd get some answers by the end of the day. "But maybe you'll find something on the video this time. This guy's bound to make a mistake sooner or later."

She nodded thoughtfully. "I was thinking last night and remembered Ricky did say something in passing about a girl he met at one of the local nightclubs. But I'm sure he didn't say her name. And I didn't really give it much credence. I mean, if he was seeing someone seriously I'd be interested in meeting her, but meeting a girl at a nightclub isn't a big deal."

He thought about that for a moment. "You mentioned Tayron asked you out all the time. When's the last time you saw him?"

She wrinkled her nose and flipped the omelet. "I think it was about a month ago that I saw Ricky and Tayron. Ricky met up with me prior to a gaming event at The Center and of course Tayron tagged along."

A tingle of excitement slipped down his spine. "Ricky and Tayron both go to The Center with you and your friends?"

"Not often, but they've gone a couple of times. Ricky was interested, but Tayron was bored by the whole thing. And he always made comments about how beautiful I was, asking why I wouldn't give him a chance." She shook her head. "I always tried to be nice, but that last time, I got super annoyed and told him to get out and leave me alone once and for all."

No wonder she'd thought Tayron Lee was the one behind her stabbing incident. Telling him off in front of others was motive for an attack.

But would someone without advanced tech skills be able to create a snow-globe bomb or elude so many of the city's cameras?

"I'd like to stay here again tonight, if that's okay."

Eden put their omelets on two plates and brought them over to the table. "I'd like that, thanks." She sat and bowed her head. He did, too.

"Dear Lord, thank you for this food we are about to eat and for keeping us safe in Your care. Amen."

"Amen," he echoed.

She glanced up at him in surprise. "I didn't realize you were a churchgoer."

"Used to be." He shifted uncomfortably in his seat. "I haven't attended since Jessica died."

Her dark eyes filled with empathy. "It's hard, isn't it? I felt the same way after losing my father to cancer, then my mother to a heart attack. But in the end, I found comfort in being in church, and in prayer."

"Jessica was the one who introduced me to God and faith." He pushed the words through his tight throat. "Afterward, I found it difficult to believe in Him."

"We all stumble in our faith at times." She reached over and lightly rested her hand on his forearm. He could feel the warmth of her fingers through the sleeve of his uniform. "But it's important to remember that God is there for us, no matter what. And that we need Him the most when we hit a rough patch."

He covered her hand with his. "I can only promise to try."

"That's all I can ask." She squeezed his arm, then withdrew her hand to pick up her fork. "I hope you like it."

"Looks great." He used the edge of his fork to cut off a piece. Flavor exploded on his tongue. "Wow, this is amazing. What's in here?"

Eden's bright smile warmed his heart. She playfully shook her finger at him. "Oh, no. I'm not revealing my culinary secrets."

Max chuckled and wondered if the food was really that great or if it was the woman seated across the table that made it special. Either way, he found himself loathe to leave.

But they both had work to do. Not to mention, he needed to stop at home to shower and change. May as well pack a bag, too, along with bringing supplies for Sam, since he would be staying here until they'd found and arrested the man responsible for these attacks on Eden. And on Patti Wang.

He glanced again at the brightly lit Christmas tree tucked in the corner of the living room, protected by the baby gate. Strange that he'd found the lights comforting last night considering he didn't have a single Christmas decoration up at his place.

Was he getting over losing Jessica? Until now, he hadn't planned to get involved in another relationship. Yet in the span of two days, he was beginning to feel at home with Eden.

Comfortable with her in a way that was completely unexpected.

And a little terrifying.

"I really hope I can find something on the video," Eden said with a sigh. "It's bugging me that this guy has managed to elude us for so long."

Eden's comment pulled him from his turbulent thoughts. "We will. As I said, he'll make a mistake soon. And I'm hoping the bomb squad turns up more information that could help. We also issued a BOLO on Tayron Lee last night based on the attack on Patti Wang."

"I feel very guilty about that. I really hope she didn't suffer because of me."

"Hey, the guy who attacked her is to blame, not you."

"Maybe." Her dark brown eyes mirrored her doubt.

They'd just finished eating when Max's phone rang. He reached over to put the call on speaker. "Santelli."

"This is Officer Hurtz with NYPD. We've got information on your BOLO, Tayron Lee."

"You found him?" Max couldn't restrain his excitement.

"Kind of," Hurtz said wryly. "We got word from Atlantic City that he and a guy by the name of Ricky Chang were both arrested two days ago for assault and battery and public intoxication."

The assault and battery charges were believable, but he frowned at the timing. "Two days ago? Are you sure?"

"One hundred percent," Hurtz said. "They were arrested at twenty-three hundred hours on Tuesday night and were about to be released this morning, until the officers saw your BOLO. There's been a request to have them transported to Brooklyn. They should be there in a few hours."

His gaze clashed with Eden's. Being arrested two days ago meant that Tayron Lee couldn't have been the one who'd followed and attempted to stab Eden or made a snow-globe bomb or attacked Patti Wang.

Which left them right back where they'd started.

SEVEN

Her assailant wasn't Tayron Lee.

Eden placed her palms on the table to keep herself centered. All this time, she'd felt certain the man following her, who'd tried to stab her, who'd put peanut oil on her salad, had to be Tayron Lee.

The idea that there was someone else out there who wanted to hurt her was staggering. And worse, Tayron had dragged her brother into something that had landed them both in jail.

"Thanks, I'll be in touch soon." Max disconnected from the call. "Eden? Are you okay?"

She tried to nod but couldn't seem to move.

"Eden?" Max's tone resonated with concern. He came over to put his hands on her shoulders, as if afraid she'd topple off her chair. "It's okay. We'll get to the bottom of this."

The warmth from his hands helped steady her. She drew in a deep breath and let it out slowly. "I know. I just thought for sure..." She couldn't finish.

A flash of guilt hit hard. All this time she'd allowed her personal feelings to taint her thoughts on the investigation. She'd actually blamed Tayron for something he didn't do.

Granted, his alibi was being in jail. But still.

She reached up and covered Max's hand with hers. "Do you think questioning them will yield any information? What could they know about what is going on here when they were in Atlantic City?"

"We still need to understand the time-line of when they left town and find out the last time your brother saw Patti Wang. Once we tie up that end, we can move on to other suspects."

"Okay, then we'd better get to work." She forced herself to push away from the table.

Max released her and she instantly missed his touch.

Stay focused, she warned herself. *You've already made one mistake. No need to add another.*

After leaving her apartment, they took a different route to Max's place. She waited in the living room with Sam as Max showered and changed into a clean uniform. His apartment was smaller than hers, but neat and tidy. What struck her the most was the stark interior without the barest hint of a personal touch.

Not a Christmas decoration to be found.

Max was likely still grieving over his dead fiancée. Any interest he may have in her was nothing more than a rebound from his self-imposed isolation.

Something she needed to remember the next time she felt the urge to kiss him. She didn't want to read more into what was going on between them. He was a coworker helping to keep her safe from harm. The last thing she needed was to open herself up to heartache.

Less than twenty minutes later, Max had

packed a bag, including supplies for Sam, and announced he was ready to go. They rode the subway to the precinct without incident and he walked her inside.

"We'll meet again for lunch," Max said, telling her rather than asking. "Please don't go anywhere alone, okay?"

"I won't. What are you going to do?"

"I'm going to check out the real-estate office, see if anyone remembers anything fishy from last night before Patti was attacked. Once Tayron and Ricky are back, I'll interview them."

"Okay." She forced a smile. "I'll review the video, see if there's a clear image of Patti's attacker."

"We have a plan." The dimple in Max's left cheek flashed. "Let me know if you find anything."

"I will." She stood for a moment, watching as Max and Sam left. As she turned, she caught Penny's speculative gaze.

"He's been a good friend," she said, trying to downplay whatever thoughts were going through Penny's head.

"Of course," Penny agreed. "It's nice to

see Max smiling more, too. Are you both planning to attend Bradley and Sasha's wedding on Christmas Eve?" Penny's older brother, Bradley MacGregor, a detective at the K-9 Unit, was marrying a local journalist.

"Um, I'm going to stop in for the reception after work, not sure about Max." She hadn't thought that far ahead; Christmas Eve was a week away. Would she see Max there? Maybe, but she didn't want to think about that too closely. "Catch you later, Penny."

She headed up to her third-floor workspace and shed her coat. Setting her personal laptop off to the side, she logged into the K-9 Unit network and began pulling up video feeds.

It didn't take long for her to find Patti Wang leaving the real-estate office at roughly eight thirty last night. She was startled to notice how Patti had been wearing a red coat similar to hers and had the same long dark hair.

Still, there were some obvious differences. Patti was taller and wore a pair of red earmuffs along with knee-high black boots. Was Max wrong about the attack being a diversion? Maybe there was someone out there who really was attacking Chinese women.

She shivered and continued following Patti as she approached the subway station. A man dressed in black followed several paces behind. When she zoomed in to get a better look at his face, she saw he was wearing a hat pulled low and had a scarf covering the lower half of his face.

It had to be the same man who'd attacked her, but she couldn't be absolutely sure until she pulled up both video feeds, the one from her attack and the more recent one, and compared them side by side.

She stared for several long moments, then caught her breath. There was a small tear along the left cuff of the guy's black jacket.

The same tear was visible in both videos.

Definitely the same man. Her pulse kicked up a notch. Now if she could only figure out who he was. The facial features were too obscured to make out the size of his nose, or his eyes. Honestly, he could have been just about anyone. There was a hint of dark hair peeking out from beneath the cap, but hair dye was cheap.

And it was eerie the way he seemed to know exactly where all the cameras were located. Which unfortunately made her think about her friends in the Geek Quad and the way they enjoyed hacking into various systems.

She saved all the video segments into a new file labeled with Patti Wang's name. Then she returned to the camera angles that displayed the coffee shop, fast-food restaurant and drugstore, backing up the video to see what had happened earlier in the evening.

She found their perp coming out of the fast-food restaurant about an hour after she and Max had left the precinct the night before. Had he realized they'd slipped past him? Had he gotten upset and taken his anger out on Patti Wang as some sort of substitute for her?

If so, what were the chances that he'd known Patti had been her brother's former girlfriend? A coincidence? Or something more sinister?

In each image she was easily able to identify the slight tear in the left cuff of his jacket, confirming it was the same suspect.

She watched the video until her vision blurred, forcing her to take a break. Walking around her office, she tried to think of another way to figure out who this guy was.

Her phone rang, and her heart leaped when she saw the caller was Max. "Hi, Max."

"I just finished with Tayron and Ricky. Unfortunately, they didn't give me much. Ricky claims he hasn't seen Patti in four months, which matches her story."

"Okay, so now what?" She tried to mask her disappointment. "I was able to get one detail from the guy's jacket. He has a very small tear along the cuff of his left sleeve. I've been able to confirm the same guy attacked me and Patti."

"Interesting. One thing Ricky did mention was that Patti had several pictures of them together on her social media pages." Max paused, then added, "Could be our guy stumbled across that information and targeted her on purpose."

"Which is exactly why I don't have a social media presence," Eden said with a sigh. "I guess you're right about the fact that I'm still the primary target."

"Yes, but we'll keep you safe, Eden. Listen, I'm hoping to finish up here within the hour. If you're interested in getting something to eat, I can pick something up on my way back."

She didn't like the thought of staying cooped up inside. "Why don't we return to the 646? We can bring pictures of our guy and question the staff again."

There was a long pause before Max said, "Okay. I'll be there as soon as I can."

"Later." She disconnected from the call and stared out through the windows overlooking the back of the building. It was a small consolation the guy sitting across the street and watching the front of the precinct couldn't see her office.

Being cooped up never bothered her before, so she told herself to get over it. Time to go back to work.

The tear in the cuff was one thing, but they'd need far more in order to figure out exactly who this guy was and why he wanted to cause her harm.

It was disappointing to admit that interviewing Tayron and Ricky had been a complete bust. It had to be done in order to fully cross the two off the list, but he'd hoped for more. For something that might lead them to the identity of this unknown stalker.

He met Eden at the precinct and waited until she'd printed a couple of photos of their suspect to show the staff at the 646 Diner. They left through the back door again, staying away from the front of the building.

Sam sniffed at various things along the way. His K-9 partner didn't alert on anything, but it didn't hurt to be careful.

"Hey, Joe." He flagged down the owner of the diner.

"Did you get my message?" Joe Best asked as he approached.

"What message?" He pulled out his cell

phone and realized he had a missed call. "Sorry, no. What's going on?"

Joe scowled and rubbed his jaw. "One of my cooks left early yesterday because he claimed he didn't feel well, but also didn't show up for work this morning. He didn't call or answer when I tried to contact him. It might be nothing, but I thought the timing was odd considering how he'd been fine until you questioned everyone."

He reached for his notebook. "What's his name?"

"Hank Voight." Joe's expression was grim. "If I find out he had anything to do with hurting Eden, I'll arrest him myself."

Max didn't bother pointing out the former cop no longer carried a badge. He pulled the photograph from his pocket and showed it to Joe. "We were able to catch a glimpse of this guy leaving through the back alley. Do you think this Hank guy allowed him in?"

Joe shook his head. "If Hank allowed him in, others would have seen him. But he may have been paid to put the peanut oil on the salad."

"I'd like to question the staff again, just to be sure. And we'll send a couple of uniforms to Hank's place."

Joe gave him Hank's address and Max called Sarge to make the request. Then he went into the kitchen to talk to the staff. After questioning everyone again, no one admitted to seeing the guy in black. However, one of the employees mentioned how Hank had gone out back in the middle of the lunch rush for a quick break, returning after a few minutes. The news was sobering.

"I'm sorry, Max. I feel like this is my fault." Joe blew out an angry breath. "Hank has worked here for six months now and seemed to fit in."

"We don't know for sure he's involved," Max cautioned. "But it does look suspicious. The peanut oil came from somewhere."

"But I don't like thinking it was my employee rather than some random customer." Joe's scowl deepened. "If he's involved…"

"We'll take care of it," Max finished

firmly. "Now how about getting us something to eat? I'm in the mood for a Reuben."

"I'll have a grilled chicken wrap," Eden said, taking one of the two open seats on the side at the counter. Sam lay down, munching on the biscuit Max had given him.

"I'll make your lunches myself and won't take my eyes off yours, Eden, until I bring the plates out."

Eden thanked him, and she and Max both kept careful watch of who came in and out of the diner.

As they finished their meals, Max's phone rang. He recognized the number of the local precinct. "Santelli."

"We found Hank Voight, looks a little green but I think that's because we're on to him rather than his claim of being too sick to work. You want to talk to him?"

"Absolutely. We'll be right there." He disconnected and gestured for the bill. "We have to run. Hank has been brought in for questioning."

Joe's eyes narrowed. "Wish I could come with you. Tell you what, your meals are on the house. It's the least I can do if Hank is responsible."

"It's not your fault, Joe." He tucked a twenty-dollar bill beneath his plate and stood. Sam eagerly jumped up to his feet, anxious to get on the move.

They walked to the K-9 Unit, heading toward the back side of the building, when Sam began to growl low in his throat.

Max abruptly stopped, raking his gaze over the area. "What is it, boy?"

Sam's nose was in the air, and the low growls continued. The tiny hairs on the back of his neck stood up as he realized danger was near.

"What's wrong with Sam?" Eden's tone held an underlying note of anxiety.

"I don't know." Max put his arm around Eden's shoulders, drawing her close. He wondered if maybe Sam had picked up on the assailant's scent, but the only place he'd been exposed to it was outside Eden's apartment door and at the precinct front desk.

Had Sam caught the guy's scent? Or that of an explosive device? "Seek, Sam. Seek."

The K-9 lifted his nose higher, trying to capture the scent.

He drew Eden close to the apartment building to keep out of the way of other pedestrians moving along the sidewalk. Scanning the area, he tried to think about where a bomb might be hidden.

Although, there was no guarantee the assailant had planted one. For all he knew, the guy had a weapon trained on them.

His gaze landed on two small Christmas trees with twinkling lights set in potted planters on either side of the entrance to the building located just a couple of yards ahead.

Max took Sam off leash. "Seek! Seek!"

Sam took a circuitous route, his nose working, until he abruptly altered right in front of the Christmas tree planter closest to them.

Fear gripped him. "Come, Sam!"

The dog whirled around and returned to his side. Using his radio, Max called for backup and the bomb squad.

"Are you sure?" Eden whispered in horror.

"Sam's got the best nose around." Max

waved his hand and shouted, "Everyone clear the area! I repeat, clear the area! Police business. I need you to step back and clear the area."

Pedestrians gaped at him, then began backing away. But they weren't moving fast enough. Eden shouted at them, too, but they still didn't seem to understand the gravity of the situation.

"Sam, Speak!"

The sturdy Rottweiler let out several sharp barks. The impact was instantaneous. People scattered, giving them and the entire area a wide berth.

"Now what?" Eden's voice had steadied, and she looked ready to do her part.

Every cell in his body wanted Eden out of danger, but he couldn't help but think this could be nothing more than another diversion. That the assailant was out there somewhere, waiting for a chance to get Eden alone.

"Backup will be here shortly, along with the bomb squad." He eyed the planter, wondering when the device would detonate. He drew Eden and Sam back a few steps, tucking them behind him. He didn't dare go too far from the source of the bomb, as he also needed to keep the public out of harm's way.

Please, God, keep us all safe in Your care.

The prayer was instinctive; he had to trust in God's will. Hearing the wail of sirens, he mentally urged them to hurry.

The seconds ticked by slowly. When the first squad arrived, double-parking a few yards ahead of where he stood, he still didn't move.

"Where is it?" one of the NYPD officers asked.

"The base of that Christmas tree. Help me secure the perimeter."

"Done." The two officers flanked him on either side, shooing the gawkers back.

"Eden, I want you to get into their squad car." He glanced over his shoulder at her. "You'll be safe there."

She looked as if she wanted to argue, but then nodded and lightly jogged toward the police vehicle. When she slipped into the back seat, he told himself to relax. But he couldn't. It wasn't far enough away, but at least she'd be safe there for the moment.

As long as the bomb didn't go off.

EIGHT

Eden watched through the passenger side window of the squad car as Max, Sam and the additional officers took charge of the scene. The bomb squad set up a cushioned barrier between the officers and the building, then used a robot device to approach the planter.

She held her breath as the robot had a steel head on it that raised and lowered. It was hard to see, but eventually the pincher end of the robot pulled a small package wrapped in dark green paper from the planter.

A sick feeling settled in her stomach. Was it possible that bomb had been meant for her? She thought back, retracing their steps. Even if they'd left from the front of the building, rather than the back, they would still go past the building.

The only way to have avoided the planter was to have gone around to the alley behind the restaurant.

But if the bomb was meant for her, why hadn't it been detonated? Had they found it too quickly? Maybe he thought they were too far away to do much damage? She buried her face in her trembling hands. Why? Who was doing this and why? While the bomb may have been intended for her, she knew that it would have hurt dozens of others, too.

Innocent bystanders, who had nothing to do with this.

Dear Lord, help us find the answers we need to keep us all safe.

There was a light tapping on her window, causing her to jerk upright. Her pulse settled when she recognized Max.

He opened the door and knelt in front of her, his gaze full of concern. Sam sat, too, as if intent on offering his support. "Are you okay?"

She forced a smile. "I will be. I'm just glad no one was hurt."

"Me, too." He held her gaze for a long moment, and it was all she could do not to throw herself into his arms. "Officer Neely is going to give you a ride back to the precinct."

"What about you and Sam?"

Max glanced at his partner. "We still need to head over to interview Hank Voight. In the meantime, I'd like you to go back to that video, see if you can see our perp leaving the bomb in the planter and/or doing a handoff with anyone from the 646."

She blew out a breath, realizing he was right. They each had a job to do and finding their bomb-planting assailant was at the top of the list. "All right. But will you please call me after your interview with Hank? I'd like to know if he gives you something to go on."

"I will." His dimple flashed. "I promise."

She reached over to lightly stroke Sam's fur. "I'm so thankful for Sam's incredible nose."

The K-9 leaned into her caress.

"That makes two of us." Max briefly covered her hand with his, then rose to his feet. "Come, Sam."

She felt certain the K-9's dark eyes held disappointment as he left her side to follow Max back to the bomb scene.

"Ready, ma'am?"

"Of course."

Officer Neely was a nice enough guy. He chatted nonstop on the short drive to the K-9 Unit, but Eden didn't hear a word he said.

Her mind was preoccupied by the near miss. And she wondered why in the world the assailant hadn't detonated the device.

Because there were too many people around? Or because he'd been waiting for the perfect time to do the maximum amount of damage?

Neither theory was reassuring.

"Eden?" The officer was looking at her expectantly.

She realized he'd parked in the angled space right in front of the doorway to their precinct. "Oh, sorry. Thanks." She pushed open the door and climbed out of the car.

Resisting the urge to glance back over her shoulder, she hurried inside.

"Eden!" Penny's eyes were wide with fear. "I'm so glad you're okay. Where's Max and Sam?"

"Max took Sam to interview someone possibly connected. They'll be here soon." She paused near Penny's desk. "If it weren't for Sam's keen nose, things could have turned out very differently."

"I know." Penny's expression turned grim. "Sarge wants this guy found ASAP."

So did she. "I'm heading up to review the video. Maybe this time, he's slipped up enough to give us a glimpse of his face."

"I hope so." Penny waved a hand. "Go and be prepared for a visit from Sarge."

Eden hurried up to her workspace, determined to have something to show Gavin and Max. This guy had to make a mistake sooner or later.

Preferably sooner.

But when she pulled up the video feed, a spear of disappointment stabbed deep. She found the man dressed in black easily enough, even pinpointed the slight tear in the cuff of his jacket. But as before, he seemed to know where the cameras were located, and used pedestrian traffic to his advantage. She could tell he approached the building where the planter was located but couldn't capture an image of him actually dropping the bomb inside. Instead, within seconds he was walking away.

She continued following his path, jumping from one video camera to the next. He kept his head down the entire time, until he finally ducked into a shop approximately a half mile from where he'd left the bomb. She continued looking to capture him leaving, but never saw him.

Which was very strange. Why hadn't he come out of the store?

"Eden?"

Gavin's voice drew her gaze from the screens before her. She nodded in acknowledgment. "Hi, Sarge. I have him on camera dropping the bomb, then going inside a store, but that's about it. He never came out and there's no clear image of his face."

Her boss stood beside her, taking in the images she'd captured on each of the four computer screens. His jaw was granite hard. "Who is this guy?"

She shook her head. "I wish I knew."

Gavin swung to face her. "You're absolutely sure you don't know him?"

"Hard to say without a good view of his face. I mean, look at that." She waved her hand at the screens. "He's average height and weight, no distinguishing marks visible. Nothing but this tiny tear in the cuff of his sleeve."

"Where?"

She used the cursor of the computer mouse to indicate the mark she'd been able to capture. Gavin leaned closer to the computer with a frown. "It's pretty small."

"But visible in each of the images." Using her keyboard, she drew up the previous videos she'd saved.

After viewing them all, Gavin nodded and stepped back. "It's something, but we could use more."

"I know. I'm trying." She didn't have to point out that she wanted this guy caught and tossed behind bars more than anyone.

Except Max.

Gavin's tone gentled. "Don't worry, we'll find him. Once Max finishes up with the bomb scene, he'll interview Hank Voight, the guy who we believe put the peanut oil on your salad. Could be he'll give us something to go on."

"I hope so. I'm going to review that video, too, see if there's footage of the handoff between my stalker and Voight in the alley behind the diner."

"Good." Gavin gave a curt nod. "Let me know if you catch them in the act."

"Yessir." She turned her attention back to her screens with a new sense of urgency. There had to be some way to crack this case open. She found a view of the alley behind the diner and saw that the man in black approached Hank Voight, the cook. It looked as if something exchanged hands, but it happened so fast it was difficult to see. Still, she sent a quick text to Max about what she'd found.

Scanning the video again, she furrowed her brow when she noticed the guy in black lightly pat his thigh with one hand as he walked. Something niggled at the back of her memory. Had she seen that gesture before?

Going through her previous video feeds, she found the guy again, this time as he left to follow Patti Wang. There! He did that same patting gesture again.

Was the gesture significant? A nervous tick? Or patting his pocket to make sure he still had something in there? It wasn't easy to tell from the grainy photos, but she found he'd done the same patting gesture again after dropping off the package containing the snow-globe bomb outside the precinct.

She sat back in her chair, her gaze moving from one screen to the next, looking at the weird pat-pat-patting again.

There was something odd about the way he did that.

But for the life of her, she couldn't figure out what it meant.

When the scene was cleared and the bomb secured in a safe hold, Max felt it was well past time to move on to the next step of the investigation.

First and foremost he wanted a vehicle.

The precinct where Hank was being de-
tained was on the other side of Brooklyn
and the sooner he could question the cook
from the 646, the better.

This was the most promising lead they
had, and he was banking on the fact that
Hank would provide a decent description
of the guy. Maybe even work with a sketch
artist to get a likeness for them to work
from.

They needed a break, soon. Before more
innocent lives were put in danger.

Especially Eden. It bothered him just
how close they'd come to the bomb site.
He reached over to pat Sam on the head.
His partner had come through for them.

"Good boy," he praised, as they headed
back to pick up a K-9 vehicle.

It was tempting to take a few minutes to
go up and see Eden, but he squelched the
urge. He was already running later than
planned. And frankly there was no reason
to see her.

Other than to reassure himself she was
really okay.

He gave himself a mental shake. Before

the attempted stabbing, he wouldn't have thought twice about it. Eden had been a valued member of their team, and nothing more.

But not any longer. She was important to him on a personal level.

He couldn't allow his preoccupation with her welfare to get in the way of doing his duty.

Twenty minutes later, he parked his SUV, took Sam out of the back, and headed inside the precinct. He offered his badge for inspection and was led into one of their interview rooms.

An officer hovered in the doorway. "Where have you been? I was getting ready to cut him loose."

"Sorry, but there was an IED situation that held me up. Hopefully this won't take long."

The officer shrugged. "Okay, I'll get Voight."

The cop returned with Hank a few minutes later. The moment Hank saw Sam, the cook shied away.

"No dogs! Get him out of here! He might attack me."

"He won't," Max said. He gave Sam a hand signal and the Rottweiler dropped to his haunches, although his gaze never left Hank. "See? He's very well trained." He pulled out a chair and sat down, pinning Hank with a stern look. After going through the Miranda warning, he asked, "Are you willing to talk to me?"

Hank shrugged. "I guess."

"Good." Max leaned forward, resting his elbows on the table. "Why did you do it?"

"Do what?" Hank feigned innocence.

Max leaned forward. "We have video that shows a man dressed in black leaving the back of the diner. We know he gave you the peanut oil with instructions to put it on Eden's food. I want to understand why you did it."

Hank seemed to shrink farther into his seat, his gaze darting around the room as if looking for a way to escape. "Are you sure it's me on that video?"

"Why didn't you go to work today?"

Hank blinked, then licked his lips. "I'm sick."

"Did he pay you?"

Hank began to nod, then caught himself. "I don't know what you're talking about."

Sam growled low in his throat.

"Okay! I put the peanut oil on her salad. I didn't think she'd stop breathing or anything. The guy said it was a joke! That she didn't like the taste, nothing more. I'm sorry, please, I'm sorry." His wide eyes were full of fear and regret.

Knowing Hank had done the deed wasn't enough. "How much did he pay you?"

"Five hundred bucks." Hank morosely stared down at the table. "I knew it was too good to be true."

"Did you know this guy? Had you seen him before?"

Hank shook his head. "Never. He just flashed the money in my face and told me he needed a favor. I was taking a quick smoke break. Joe doesn't like it, but it's stressful back there in the middle of the lunch rush. I had a quick smoke and this guy asked me to use the peanut oil as a practical joke on his friend. I needed the cash, so I took it."

Friend? "Describe him for me."

Now Hank looked confused. "Describe him?"

Max tamped down a flash of impatience. "Race, hair color, eye color, age, scars or other identifiable features."

"Um, white. And, um, average height and weight. Maybe dark hair. I couldn't see much of his face, because he had a scarf and wore a hat."

Max couldn't stand the thought that he'd run into another dead end. "Tell me exactly what he said."

Hank licked his lips again. "He said, 'Do you want to make a quick five hundred bucks? I need you to put this peanut oil on my friend's food—she's sitting with a cop at the end of the counter. It's a private joke.'"

Max replayed the statement in his mind. The guy must have seen him and Eden go in and sit down together. "Was the peanut oil in a container of some sort?"

"Yeah." Hank glanced between them. "I

squirted some on and then tossed it in a dumpster in the alley. Look, I'm sorry. The five hundred bucks wasn't worth all this."

No, it wasn't. Max gestured for the officers to go check out the dumpsters behind the restaurant. Finding the bottle would be good, although likely not helpful as the assailant had been wearing gloves.

On his way back to the precinct, his phone rang. "Santelli."

"Max? It's Darcy. The bomb squad uncovered the phone number that was programmed in to detonate the snow-globe device."

"Really? That's great news. What's the number? We need to find out who owns the phone associated with it."

"We already know," Darcy said. "It's Eden's cell number."

"Eden's?" He tightened his grip on the steering wheel. "Are you sure?"

"Yes."

"Thanks." He disconnected from the call, trying not to imagine Eden using her phone near the snow globe only to have it blow up in her face. She collected snow globes. Chances are that she'd have put it on her desk. How many times did she use her phone during any given day? Probably too many.

This wasn't your average bomb freak. This level of skill was at a much higher level.

And he had no idea when this guy would try to strike next.

NINE

Eden rubbed her blurry eyes and stepped away from her workstation. Her head ached, and she felt sick to her stomach.

Max wouldn't be here yet for another hour, even though it was past five o'clock in the evening. They were no closer to finding out who had targeted her and why. Except for the latest news about her cell phone being the trigger of the snow-globe bomb, they had nothing more to go on, even after questioning Hank Voight.

The cell-phone trigger bothered her, making it difficult to concentrate on the video. Deep down, she knew the person responsible could be one of her Geek Quad friends. They were experts at hacking, and the attacks seemed so personal.

But why?

Bryon, Tom and Darnell had been her close friends since high school and through college. They all had high-level government jobs. It made no sense that one of them would have some sort of personal grudge against her.

Just thinking about the possibility that one of her longtime friends had turned on her to the point they wanted to harm her, or worse, kill her, filled her with a horrible sense of dread.

She stared sightlessly out the window, trying to come up with an alternate and less disturbing theory. Lots of people had amazing tech skills. Lots of people could create a bomb. But putting the two together, as far as using technology to detonate a bomb, would require a particular skill set.

Whirling around, she crossed over to her workstation and shut it down. Pulling her prized laptop out of the shoulder bag, she booted it up. When she opened her email, she noticed the government recruiter had sent another message, asking if she'd considered moving forward with an interview.

She couldn't imagine changing jobs right

now. Maybe something to think about after the holiday. Ignoring that message, she scanned the texts in her messaging app. There was a group message from Tom asking if they were still on for Monday. Bryon had replied yes, but there was nothing from Darnell yet.

Feeling determined, she opened the text and replied all to count her in for Monday's gathering. After hitting Send, she sat back and wondered if the fact that Darnell hadn't responded was because he was preoccupied with planting bombs.

Or maybe it was Tom who was trying to deflect suspicion by sending the message in the first place, pretending to be all casual about their next get-together.

But why? That was the big stumbling point for her. Not one of the guys had ever looked at her with romantic interest. In fact, the last time they'd gotten together, Tom mentioned meeting a woman he was interested in seeing again. And Bryon had been dating someone for several months. What was her name? Rachel? No, Rochelle. Darnell had chimed in about his preference of playing the field.

None of it made any sense.

As soon as she'd responded, Darnell replied, adding his agreement. Tom ended the conversation saying he'd see them all on Monday.

Today was Friday. Monday was three days away.

When she joined her friends at The Center, would she be looking into the eyes of a killer?

She shivered and turned her attention to the recruiter email. Hitting Reply, she told him to contact her again after Christmas. Part of her felt bad for stringing him along, but she knew the smart thing would be to keep her options open.

"Eden? Are you ready to go?"

Max's low voice had her glancing up in surprise. His warm and weary smile caused her pulse to kick up. "Hi, Max."

"Sorry it took longer than I thought to get here." His gaze darkened with concern. "Thanks for waiting for me."

"Sarge's orders, right?" She strove for a casual tone, but Max frowned.

"Eden, I'm here because I want to be." He stepped closer. Even after a long day, his sandalwood scent had the ability to knock her off balance. "I want you protected."

"Thanks, I appreciate that." Their gazes clung and held for a long breathless moment. Max bent his head to kiss her, at the same moment Sam nudged her with his nose. Max grimaced and moved back, making her laugh as she reached down to stroke his soft fur. "You're a good boy, Sam."

"With rotten timing," Max muttered.

She smiled again, feeling much better now that Max and Sam were there. It was difficult to remember how she'd always headed home alone without thinking twice about it.

Spending time with Max was nice. She'd miss being close to him once they caught this guy.

After shutting down her computer, she tucked it back into her bag and drew the strap over her head so that the bag was resting crosswise against her. Max held her coat for her, and she gratefully placed her arms in the sleeves and allowed him to pull it up over her shoulders. His broad hands rested there for a minute before releasing her. She sensed him stepping away.

They didn't say much on the way down to the main level of the precinct. There was a second-shift clerk seated behind the desk, but the other cubicles were empty.

Once again, Max steered her through to the back exit of the building.

"Don't you think this guy has figured out we leave this way?" She caught her breath at the blast of cold December air hitting her face.

"Maybe, but there are less places for him to hide." Max and Sam stayed close to her side.

They headed toward the subway, choosing the same entrance as the day before. She almost asked about taking a rideshare instead but decided against it. It was possible that some rideshare drivers would balk at having Sam in the vehicle. He was a large and intimidating animal. She could see how many might view him as scary.

"Are you interested in stopping for a bite to eat?" Max asked, as they came down the steps toward the turnstile.

She wasn't at all hungry but nodded. "Whatever you'd like is fine."

Before he could respond, there was a shout from a woman standing several feet ahead of them. "Help! It's a bomb! Someone help!"

"What in the world?" Max's tone was grim as they both noticed the large backpack sitting beneath the bench. "Who told you it's a bomb?"

The woman waved a handwritten note. "He—he gave me this and left. It says the backpack is a bomb!"

Not again! Please, Lord, not again!

"Everyone stay back," Max ordered, reaching up for his radio. Masses of people moved away from the backpack, heading toward the stairway they'd just come down, jostling her as they passed.

"I need this train line and station shut down. Send me backup and the bomb squad ASAP." Max released the leash from Sam's collar. "Seek, Sam. Seek!"

She was watching Sam alert on the backpack when she felt something sharp poke her in the back. "Stay quiet, or I'll blow up the dog."

Every muscle in her body went still. The voice was a low whisper, but she felt certain it was familiar. She held her breath, afraid to do anything that would cause Sam or Max harm.

"Come with me." The man drew her backward. She stumbled as she attempted to do what he asked, her gaze boring into Max's back as she willed him to turn around, to notice she was leaving.

But all too soon, they were swallowed into the massive crowd. In addition to the stairs, there was an escalator up, jam-packed with people getting as far away from the backpack and the subway station as possible. He moved her onto the escalator, and as she glanced at the gloved hand holding tightly to her arm, she noticed the slight tear in the cuff.

No! This couldn't be happening! This guy had actually planted the bomb as a way to get to her! She tried to capture other people's gazes, but no one was paying the least bit of attention to her or the man who held her at knifepoint. She thought about trying to scream or shout but couldn't bear the thought of this guy setting off the bomb, hurting Max and Sam, not to mention dozens of other innocent lives.

Please, God, help me!

She glanced over her shoulder, trying to get a glimpse of her assailant's face. As before, he had a dark hat over his hair and a scarf pulled up to cover most of his face. But then she caught a glimpse of his eyes and instantly recognized him.

Bryon Avery. The pat-pat-patting suddenly made sense. Bryon had often displayed that nervous tick. She hadn't connected that before, maybe because she'd found it so hard to accept that one of the Geek Quad could want to hurt her.

"Why?" Her voice came out a croak. "I don't understand."

"Shut up." Bryon tightened his grip, making her wince with pain. "Don't bother playing up the innocent act with me. You know very well why I'm doing this."

"I don't!" She squeezed the words past her tight throat. "We were friends. I don't understand why you're doing this."

"I told you to shut up!" He held up his cell phone with his other hand just enough so she could see it. "Or should I go ahead and detonate the backpack?"

No! Max! Sam! She sucked in a harsh breath and bit her lip to keep from crying out. There was no doubt in her mind that Bryon would do as he threatened if she stepped out of line.

They hit the street level and he took her the same way he'd escaped that very first night. The night he'd tried to stab her. In a desperate move, she pulled off her red-knit glove and dropped it to the ground. Maybe, just maybe, Max and Sam would find it.

But as he urged her forward, farther away from Max and Sam, her despair grew, filling her with fear.

By the time Max realized she was gone, it would be too late. Bryon Avery, her one-time friend turned tormentor, would have her just where he wanted.

* * *

"Come, Sam." Max held his breath until his partner turned away from the backpack and trotted back to his side. He clipped on Sam's leash, then faced the few gawkers that remained. He needed to secure the perimeter and was irritated that some people didn't seem to have basic common sense. "Everyone get back! I want you to clear the area!"

The lingering people scattered. He scowled as he abruptly realized Eden wasn't nearby. Had she gone up to the street level to wait for his backup? The sirens were growing louder, indicating they were on the way. While a part of him was glad she was far away from the backpack bomb, he didn't like not seeing her.

"Eden?" He shouted her name, his voice echoing off the concrete walls of the subway station. "Eden!"

No response.

A tingle of fear snaked down his spine. "Eden!" He urged Sam farther from the backpack, until they were near the bottom of the stairs. He looked up, hoping to see her, but there was no sign of her red coat.

Where was she? Max pulled out his cell phone to call her, then hesitated and glanced at the backpack. What if the stupid thing was set to detonate when she used her cell phone?

Shoving the phone back into his pocket, he reached for his radio, getting in touch with the desk clerk at their Brooklyn K-9 precinct. "This is Santelli. I need to be connected with Danielle Kowalski from the NYC K-9 Command Unit in Queens, ASAP. I need her to locate Eden Chang."

"Eden's missing? Hang on." There was a moment of silence before he was patched through to the Queens unit.

"This is Danielle."

"Officer Santelli from Brooklyn. I believe Eden has been abducted from the Bay Ridge subway station by an assailant dressed in black. I need you to get eyes on her."

"Okay, give me a sec."

He tightened his grip on the radio, feeling certain they didn't have a second to waste.

He tried to estimate how much time had gone by. Ten minutes? Fifteen? He wasn't sure. As much as he wanted to instantly follow her, he couldn't leave the stupid backpack bomb unattended.

Where was the bomb squad? They should have been here by now.

"I think I see her," Danielle's voice sounded hesitant. "They're heading north down the street away from the subway station."

They? Max realized the perp was taking the same route as he had the night of the stabbing. "Keep your eyes on her," he ordered. "Is anyone close enough to tail her?"

"Not yet."

"Get someone on it. As soon as my backup arrives, Sam and I will head out, too."

"I will," Danielle promised.

The reassurance didn't help him feel better. The sirens were loud enough now, indicating help had arrived. Still, it seemed to take forever for the officers to make their way toward him.

He quickly filled them in on what was going on. "I need to go after Eden."

"You can't leave," the officer protested.

Max ignored him. He jogged up the stairs to the street with Sam keeping pace at his side. He tried to think of something he could use for Sam to track her scent.

If only he'd taken her computer bag from her! He fought the wave of panic, sweeping his gaze over the area as he headed in the direction Danielle had indicated.

A red-knit glove caught his eye. Eden had been wearing red gloves. It looked relatively clean as if it hadn't been there very long. With a surge of hope, he carefully picked it up. He couldn't detect her spicy scent but knew Sam could.

He reached for his radio. "Danielle? Where's Eden? Did she drop a red glove?"

"Yes, video shows her drop the glove mere moments before she and the guy in black disappeared from view." There was a pause. "I think I've lost her, Max. I'll keep watching the cameras, but for the moment she and the man who abducted her are out of sight."

"Okay, thanks." Max stopped and held the glove out for Sam. "This is Eden. Seek Eden!"

Sam sniffed the glove for a long minute before turning back to the street. He lifted his nose in the air in a way that Max knew meant he was trying to hone in on Eden's scent.

"Seek Eden, Sam," he repeated.

Sam moved forward eagerly. Max kept him on leash but didn't hesitate to break into a jog when his partner picked up the pace.

Please, Lord, show me and Sam the way!

Sam backtracked once, then continued moving down the street. Max looked at the various shops, recognizing the ones that stayed open late from the day he'd investigated the attempted stabbing.

He felt certain Sam wouldn't let him down. That God was actually watching over them, helping to guide them down the right path.

It was impossible to imagine life without Eden, so he shut down any negative thoughts. They would find her. And she would be okay.

Sam alerted at the front door of a shop located near the end of the street. It was a touristy kind of place, the sort that sold lots of different types of trinkets from images of the Statute of Liberty to the Empire State Building.

There were even a couple of snow globes exactly like the one that had been made into a bomb and sent to Eden at the station.

His pulse shot up as he realized they were hot on this guy's trail. He pinned the counter clerk with a fierce glare. "NYPD. Which way did they go?"

"Huh?" The guy looked confused.

"I'll arrest you for aiding and abetting a criminal. Tell me which way the woman in the red coat and the guy dressed in black went!"

Sam growled as if sensing Max's frustration.

"There." The clerk lifted a shaky hand, pointing toward a narrow doorway.

He pulled the door open, finding a flight

of rickety stairs heading downward. He glanced back at the clerk. "Are you sure?"

The clerk nodded. "It leads to tunnels beneath the city."

He'd heard of the tunnels but had never been in them. Max turned on his flashlight and headed down, hoping and praying that Eden was still alive and unharmed.

TEN

"Bryon, please, tell me what's going on." Eden had dropped another glove once he'd dragged her down into the tunnels beneath the city. It was all she could think of as a way to help Max and Sam find her. But she had no idea if they were still at the bomb scene.

She'd heard of the tunnels but had never been down here. And didn't much like them now. Bryon had a small light, but she couldn't see much. The walls were dark and damp, and she feared there were rats or other creepy-crawlies surrounding them. The very idea made her shiver. When she felt something scuttle over her right foot, she swallowed a scream.

There had to be something she could do to get away from him. To get herself out of this mess. She forced the panic back so she could think. She had one more item to drop, and that was her red-knit hat. Would Bryon notice if she wasn't wearing it? Maybe not. She was beginning to think he wasn't quite sane.

"Why do you think the government is trying to recruit you?"

His abrupt question made her frown.

"I—don't know," she said.

He let out a low hiss of disgust. "Because they fired me, that's why. And I learned you were the NSA's first choice all along. Pretty, perfect Eden Chang." Venom dripped from his tone.

"I—I'm sorry to hear you lost your job. That must have been terrible." It was news to her that she'd been their first choice, but she doubted that alone had any bearing on the government's decision to fire Bryon.

He pulled her deeper into the tunnels, seemingly knowing exactly where he wanted to go. "Rochelle dumped me right after I was fired. I lost everything, and it's all your fault."

"Me?" Her voice came out in a high

squeak. "I didn't do anything. I don't even want the job." The minute she said the words, she knew they were absolutely true. Working for the NYPD's Brooklyn K-9 Unit was where her heart was.

Not to mention Max. And the other members of the team.

But mostly Max.

Lord, please help Max and Sam find me!

"Yeah, right," Bryon scoffed, as he led her deeper into the darkness and farther away from any possibility of rescue. "I heard they were going to offer you double what I was making, and it has to be far more than whatever measly salary the NYPD is paying you. Only an idiot would refuse the job."

There was more to life than money, but arguing would be useless, so she tried to switch tactics in an effort to keep him talking. "And what about Patti Wang?"

"She was nothing other than a way to throw suspicion on your brother's idiot friend. I barely scratched her."

His flat admission was terrifying. It was as if he had no empathy for others at all.

"Did you hack into the subway video feeds? Is that how you avoided the cameras?"

"I'm better than you, Eden. Too bad the NSA doesn't agree."

Keep him talking. "I still don't understand why you're trying to hurt me. I thought we were friends. I would never turn against you, Bryon."

His grip on her arm tightened painfully. "Sure you would. Besides, it's not just about you, Eden. It's about proving my worth to those idiots at the NSA."

Proving his worth? "You mean the way you created the bombs to be triggered by a specific phone number?"

"Exactly." Satisfaction rang from his tone. "Soon they'll know exactly what they missed by letting me go."

Her mouth was dry with fear at his veiled threat. "What are you planning?"

"You'll see." She didn't have to see his face to know he was smirking.

They turned down another tunnel, and Bryon slowed down as if he were searching for something. In the faint light, she could see a rickety ladder leading up, maybe to another shop much like the one they'd used to come down.

She quickly dropped her hat to let Max or Sam or anyone know which direction he'd taken her.

If Max and Sam were following at all.

No, she refused to give up her faith. God was watching over her. Max was too smart not to realize she'd been taken. And she knew in her heart he and Sam would do whatever necessary to find her.

It was her job to stay alive long enough for him to accomplish that goal.

Max could hear voices in the tunnel up ahead, but the concrete walls distorted the sound such that he couldn't quite make out what they were saying.

He was grateful they weren't too far ahead. Keeping his hand covering the head of his flashlight to douse most of the illumination, he quickened his pace, trying to come up with a plan.

Unfortunately, his phone wasn't getting service down here and using his radio would be too loud. He didn't want the perp to know how close he was. He'd given his last location to Gavin just as he entered the tunnel.

Members of his team should be there soon.

Sam abruptly stopped. He turned to see his partner had found another of Eden's red gloves. "Good boy," he whispered, giving Sam's coat a good rub. He offered the glove for Sam to sniff. "Good boy. Seek Eden."

Sam eagerly surged forward, dragging Max along with him. The voices up ahead were getting louder now, and he didn't dare delay much longer. Sam wasn't just a great bomb-sniffing K-9. He'd also attack on command.

The only concern that weighed heavily in the back of his mind was the backpack bomb. He felt certain the guy who'd grabbed Eden wouldn't hesitate to set it off. The bomb squad was there and hopefully taking care of getting the device into a safety box, but what if they hadn't managed that yet?

What if the device blew up in their faces?

He couldn't bear to think about that, so he concentrated on closing the gap.

"Please don't do this, Bryon. Think about all the innocent people who don't deserve this."

Eden's voice was clear, as if she were only a couple of yards away. Sam alerted again on her hat. Max picked it up and offered the fresh scent to Sam without speaking. He also slipped the K-9 off leash.

They turned the corner and Max caught a glimpse of light from halfway up the wall. No! They were heading up a ladder leading out of the tunnel!

"Get him!" Sam let out a series of ferocious barks, surging ahead, and grabbed the back of the guy's jacket, hanging on with his steel-trap jaws and using all his weight to hold the guy back.

Several things happened at once. The guy's head jerked back as Eden's boot lashed out, clipping his chin. The Rottweiler's strength brought the guy down several rungs, although he somehow managed to hang on.

Max let the flashlight drop, grabbed the

guy's arm and yanked hard. "Stop! You're under arrest!"

"Let me go, or I'll detonate the bomb!"

Eden kicked out again, and the perp lost his grip on the ladder, his arms flailing as he fought for balance.

Between Max and Sam, they managed to pin the guy down. From the light radiating from his flashlight, he searched for a cell phone, but the guy's hands were empty.

Which didn't mean he didn't have another way to trigger the device.

Sam continued to bark in the perp's face in a scare tactic that worked wonders. The guy—Eden had called him Bryon, which meant he was one of the Geek Quad friends—put his hands up to cover his face. "Get him off me!"

"Where's the trigger for the bomb?" Max pulled his handcuffs off his belt. Eden came down to stand beside him.

"His name is Bryon Avery and his phone's in his right pocket." She sounded breathless. "He told me he's created a way to trigger a bomb from a specific cell number."

After cuffing Avery's wrists, he searched

for and drew out the guy's cell phone, holding it gingerly by the edges as he dropped it into an evidence bag. Then he used his radio to call Gavin.

"Sam and I found Eden and have Bryon Avery in custody. What's the update with the bomb squad?"

"They have the backpack device secured. Tyler Walker and his K-9, Dusty, should be coming through the tunnel any minute."

"Max? Eden?" The detective's voice echoed off the concrete walls. "Are you okay?"

"We're fine." For a moment Max hung his head, as the magnitude of how close he'd come to losing Eden hit hard. He hadn't wanted anyone else after losing Jessica. He hadn't wanted to fall in love again.

But it was too late. His heart already belonged to Eden.

"Max? Are you okay?" Eden placed her hand on his arm, drawing his gaze.

"I'm fine, but what about you?" He raked his gaze over her. "Did he hurt you?"

"No, but he mentioned some grand plans

to make the NSA sorry for firing him. I'm worried he has more bombs planted."

Just what he didn't want to hear. "Okay, we'll have to send a notice to all precincts to be aware of any suspicious packages." He gripped Avery's arms and drew him upright. He quickly recited the Miranda warning, then asked, "Where are they? Where did you leave the bombs?"

Avery sneered. "Wouldn't you like to know."

Max had to bite back a flash of temper. "If those bombs hurt the public, you'll be looking at multiple counts of murder. Is that really what you want?"

"We need to check The Center," Eden said. "Our hangout."

The involuntary twitch at the corner of Avery's eyes betrayed him. Max grabbed his radio. "Send the bomb squad to a gaming place called The Center to search for another device." He glanced at Eden. "Where else?"

She wrinkled her forehead in concentration. "Maybe Bryon's former girlfriend's place? Her name is Rochelle Cannon."

Avery's jaw tightened and he looked away, which made Max think Eden had guessed correctly once again. He repeated the information to the dispatcher.

"What about your other Geek Quad members?" He glanced at Eden. "Could they be in danger?"

"We should have their places checked out, but it appears Bryon held me responsible for being fired. And for being recruited to take his spot."

"Recruited to take his spot?" He repeated in surprise. "I didn't know you were being recruited by the NSA."

"I didn't know the position was with the NSA. The government recruiter who contacted me didn't say much over email. He was pressing for a face-to-face interview."

An interview with a recruiter. Max didn't have any idea what to say. It never occurred to him that Eden might leave the Brooklyn K-9 Unit. Not that she wasn't talented enough to work for the NSA, because she was.

But man, he didn't want her to leave.

"Let's get this guy out of here," Tyler said,

interrupting his thoughts. "Maybe once he gets his lawyer, he'll understand that cooperating with us is the wisest option."

"Yeah." It took Max a moment to focus on their next steps. "Let's get him out of the tunnel."

No easy task as they didn't want to completely uncuff his wrists. After sending Eden up first, he and Tyler managed to carry Avery up to the main level. Sam and Dusty, a golden retriever, bounded after them.

Tyler offered to take Avery to the jail. Max called Gavin, letting him know they were heading over to check on the other possible bomb locations.

"No need. I just heard from the bomb squad. They found one device inside the gaming joint and another inside Rochelle's place. Thankfully, she wasn't home. We haven't found any other devices."

"Let's hope three devices is all he had time to set up before grabbing Eden."

"I hear you," Gavin agreed.

"I'm going to take Eden home, so Sam can make sure her place is secure."

"Good idea. I think we're finished for now, but if I need you and Sam to find another device, I'll let you know."

"Okay, thanks." He disconnected from the line. "Let's get out of here."

He called for a car service, stressing the fact that he had a police dog with him. After several declines, one driver agreed to pick them up.

"Behave," he said to Sam when the vehicle arrived.

Sam looked up at him as if to say, *Why wouldn't I?*

Once they were settled, with Sam on the floor at his feet, the driver headed to Sunset Park. Eden reached over to take his hand. "I knew you and Sam would find me."

He stared down at their entwined fingers for a long moment. "It was all I could think about once I realized you were missing. Smart of you to drop clues along the way."

A smile tugged at the corner of her mouth. "It was the least I could do. All of this—" she waved a hand "—because he was fired and blamed me? How crazy is that?"

"I should have dug deeper into your friend's backgrounds."

She arched a brow. "I'm not sure that knowing about his being let go would have been enough for me to suspect he was capable of all this."

He lifted their joined hands so he could kiss her fingers. "I prayed God would keep you safe, and He did."

A smile bloomed on her features. "Me, too. I had faith in God and in you, and of course Sam." She reached down to pet Sam's fur.

He was humbled by her response, but still couldn't get the news of the government recruiter out of his head. Should he ask about it? Or wait for her to bring it up? Was it possible she didn't feel as deeply about him as he felt about her? Or did she think taking the NSA job wouldn't be a barrier between them since most of their work was done remotely? He didn't know much about their scheduling practices. What if they couldn't get the same days off?

He fell silent as the driver navigated the crowded streets toward Sunset Park. Christmas lights twinkled from various apartments, and for the first time, he realized how much he wanted to spend some time around the holidays with Eden.

"I spoke to Ricky earlier today," Eden said. "He's upset with Tayron getting him in trouble. I'm hoping that when he's released he'll come visit me."

"That would be good for you to have your brother back."

"Yes." She smiled wryly. "I can only hope he'll stay on the straight and narrow from now on."

"All you can do is offer your support, Eden. Ricky has to make the choice to change his life." He didn't want her to feel responsible for her brother's decisions.

"I know." She hesitated, then asked, "Um, are you planning to go to Bradley and Sasha's wedding on Christmas Eve?"

Eden's question caught him off guard. "Yeah, I was going to stop by the reception after work. I signed up to staff the holiday to give those with families time off. Bradley said that dropping in at the reception would be fine."

"I was going to attend the reception, too. But—I wouldn't mind sharing a ride. If that works out for you." Eden was avoiding his direct gaze in a way that gave him a flicker of hope.

She actually wanted to go to the wedding reception with him!

"I'd love to escort you to the wedding." Was that his voice all gravelly and rough? He cleared his throat. "I wasn't looking forward to attending, but now I can't wait."

"Great." Her smile lit up her entire face, her sheer beauty hitting him squarely between the eyes.

"Hey, the address you're looking for is right over there, but I'm in a bit of a traffic jam here." The guy waved at the windshield where there was nothing but streams of red taillights stretching before them.

"Let us out here. We'll walk the rest of the way." He quickly paid the guy on his app, including an additional tip for allowing Sam to ride along.

The walk to Eden's apartment building didn't take long. As they approached her doorway, he bent down and let Sam off leash.

"Seek, Sam. Seek!"

His partner went to work, sniffing along the hallway without alerting. Even at her apartment door, he didn't pick up anything significant. Feeling reassured, Max took her key and unlocked the door. "Stay here until we clear it."

As before—had it been only a few days ago?—he and Sam went through the apartment. Charlie meowed with annoyance, but Sam ignored the tabby.

"All clear." He gestured for Eden to come inside. "Avery apparently couldn't find a good hiding spot here."

"Thankfully, he didn't have a key." She shrugged off her coat and sighed. "I never want to be in those tunnels again."

"I know." He drew her close in a warm hug, the way he'd wanted to do from the moment he found her.

She wrapped her arms around his waist and nestled against him. "Oh, Max. I'm so glad you're here with me."

The flicker of hope in his chest burned hotter. "What about that recruiter?"

She lifted her head to look into his eyes. "I put him off until after the holidays, but I can just tell him no right now. I'm not leaving the Brooklyn K-9 Unit."

Really? He stared into her dark eyes. "Because of Avery?"

She smiled and shook her head. "No, silly. Because of you. I know it's probably too soon for you to hear this, but I've fallen in love with you, Max Santelli."

He blinked, wondering if he'd misunderstood. But then she went up on her tiptoes and kissed him.

Hauling her close, he kissed her back. It was several minutes before either of them could speak.

"Eden, I love you. And it's not that fast, as I've been thinking of you for months now."

"Months? Why didn't you ask me out?"

He shook his head. "I was too afraid of getting hurt, but that was a dumb reason. My heart was already involved with you, regardless of the obstacles my brain tried to create."

She smiled and kissed him again. "I'm glad you followed your heart."

"Me, too." He drew her over to the sofa. As they sat down, the cat meowed again, dashing out of the bedroom straight toward Sam. The dog braced himself as the animal launched into the air, landing directly on Sam's broad back.

"Meow!" Charlie said again.

Sam froze, then turned his head toward Max as if silently asking for help. When none came, the K-9 lowered himself to the floor, taking care not to disturb Charlie.

"Good boy." Max chuckled. "See? I told you they'd find a way to get along."

Sam offered a baleful gaze as if agreeing to put up with this nonsense, for now.

"This is going to be a great Christmas," Max murmured, pressing a kiss to Eden's temple.

"Yes." She sighed and snuggled close. "The best Christmas ever."

* * * * *

Dear Reader,

I hope you've enjoyed your journey through the *True Blue K-9 Unit: Brooklyn* series, including Max and Eden's story. I'm blessed to work with an exceptional group of authors. Coordinating our stories through a series this size is never easy, but we always find a way—especially with our wonderful editor, Emily Rodmell, at the helm.

Thanks to everyone who took the time to send lovely notes or leave positive reviews. I appreciate my readers very much!

Christmas is a special time not just being with family and friends but understanding how important the birth of Jesus has been for the entire world. I hope you find peace, love and joy this holiday season.

Merry Christmas,
Laura Scott

PS: You can find me through my website at www.laurascottbooks.com, or

Facebook at LauraScottBooks or
Twitter @laurascottbooks.
I also offer a free novella to my
newsletter subscribers.

GIFT-WRAPPED DANGER
Maggie K. Black

With thanks to

Heather Woodhaven for her wonderful story
about Raymond and Abby, which inspired this book

and Cate Nolan
for being my writing buddy

Both are Love Inspired Suspense authors.
Go read their books. They're awesome.

Show me thy ways, O Lord. Teach me thy paths.
-Psalms 25:4

Show me thy ways, O Lord: Teach me thy paths.
—Psalms 25:4

ONE

The sights and sounds of Christmastime seemed to surround Officer Noelle Orton on all sides as she stepped inside the busy Brooklyn shopping mall with her K-9 partner, Liberty, by her side. Glittering decorations draped from the ceiling above her. Happy couples wandered hand in hand from one dazzling storefront to the next. The voices of excited families mingled with the carols being piped through the sound system. Christmas was only two days away and last-minute shoppers were out in full force. Noelle took a deep breath to quell the worry in her heart and tightened her grip on the yellow Labrador's leash, as she spotted Officer Raymond Morrow striding toward her with his springer spaniel K-9 partner, Abby. The slight frown on her fellow officer's face told her everything she needed to know in a glance.

The smuggled drugs still hadn't been found.

K-9 teams specializing in narcotic detection had fanned out at malls, stores and warehouses across New York after an investigation into a murdered dockworker at Red Hook Container Terminal led to the detection of trace amounts of the psychoactive drug MDMA—commonly known as Ecstasy or Molly—on an empty ship that had contained several containers of toys.

The mere thought that dangerous drugs might've gotten mixed up in some child's Christmas presents filled her core with urgency. Liberty whimpered softly, as if sensing Noelle's tension. Noelle ran her hand over the dog's head and scratched gently behind Liberty's left ear with its distinctive black smudge. Then she exchanged hellos with Raymond as the K-9s greeted each other, their tails wagging.

"Looks like someone is happy," Raymond

said, glancing at Liberty. "How does it feel to be back on active cases?"

"Wonderful," Noelle admitted. Noelle and Liberty had been forced to stop taking high-visibility cases for more than six months, after a vengeful gunrunner had placed a ten-thousand-dollar bounty on the exceptional dog's head. Now thankfully the gunrunner was behind bars. But as a rookie officer and former K-9 trainer, she also felt the pressure to prove to Sergeant "Sarge" Gavin Sutherland and the rest of the Brooklyn K-9 Unit team that she and Liberty hadn't gotten rusty. "You should've seen how excited Liberty was when I clipped her leash on this morning and told her it was time to go to work. She'd have dragged me to the vehicle if I'd let her. I'm guessing no fresh leads on the case?"

"Not yet." Raymond shook his head and worry darkened her fellow officer's eyes. "Last I heard, Sarge is looking for people willing to pull in extra shifts over the holidays to work this one."

"I'll talk to him," Noelle said. She wanted

as much overtime as she could get. The yellow Lab glanced up at her under furry blond eyebrows, as if to say she agreed. "Liberty and I had nothing planned but a quiet Christmas alone, just the two of us, and we're both eager to work since we were cooped up until a couple months ago. What are you going to do?"

"I talked it over with Karenna and she's game as long as we make it to Christmas Eve with my family and Christmas day with her dad," Raymond said. He and his fiancée, Karenna, had reunited during a dangerous drug case. "Especially since Sarge has already signed off on some time off for wedding planning. Karenna's dad wants to invite business contacts from around the world and make it swanky, while my mom wants an intimate Italian feast." He chuckled. "Karenna's siding with Mom, but I think it's just because my sister told her it's tradition the groom serenades the bride at the window the night before the wedding."

She chuckled along with him. As an only

child of two very driven, workaholic parents who now lived on the other side of the country, Noelle couldn't remember the last time she'd had anything close to a family-focused Christmas.

"We should split up to cover more ground," Raymond said. "Abby and I will take the big toy store at this end. Can you head to the center courtyard? There's some kind of large charity toy giveaway. Huge tree, big crowd. You can't miss it."

"We're on it," Noelle said. She said goodbye to Raymond and Abby, and silently prayed that next time they touched base it would be with good news. Noelle followed her partner as she sniffed her way through the busy mall. When they turned a corner, Liberty gave a slight tug on the leash followed by a soft woof. Hope leaped afresh in Noelle's chest. Liberty had detected something. "Show me."

The dog took off trotting, moving as quickly as Noelle would allow, following posters leading to The Jolly Family Charity Christmas Toy Giveaway. Judging by the flow of foot traffic, it seemed half the mall was heading that way too. She glanced at the poster. Well, the name was definitely a mouthful. And judging by the picture of the strong man in fatigues on the poster, Mr. Jolly was a corporal, tall, dark-haired and most definitely handsome. But did he have anything to do with the smuggled drugs?

Either way, it seemed Liberty was pulling her that way. She checked her watch. It was quarter after four now. The toy giveaway was scheduled to start at five o'clock, and already she could see families beginning to line up in the long roped-off rows that zigzagged back and forth in front of a small decorated stage. Liberty led her past the crowd and up toward the stage, where a gray-haired couple in blue jeans and festive sweaters were setting up a Christmas tree. No toys in sight though.

For a moment it looked like Liberty was leading her somewhere behind the stage. Then the dog doubled back to sniff a small pair of bright blue superhero boots attached to a pair of skinny little legs, which poked out from under a curtain near the back of the stage. Liberty continued to sniff the boots. They kicked and wriggled in response. Then a small boy, of around five years old, crawled out from under the curtain and looked down at Liberty.

"Hello, Mr. Officer Dog!" he said. "Why are you sniffing me?"

Noelle blinked. Good question. The kid had an unruly mop of black curls tucked into an oversize red jester's hat that had bells on it. His bright blue eyes looked up at Noelle keenly.

"May I pet your dog, Officer?" he asked. "Or is he on duty?"

"She's a girl," Noelle said. "Her name is Liberty, and she's on duty."

The little boy nodded. The bells jangled and a couple more curls escaped from his hat. "So no petting."

"No petting," Noelle confirmed. "But thank you for asking. That was a very smart question."

But who are you? And what do you have to do with this? A slight tug on the leash told her that whatever had made Liberty decide to give the boy a second look had passed and her partner was now ready to move on. After all, she'd been trained to dismiss trace scents. But Liberty had also definitely sensed something around the stage. Was it a false positive? Or had this little boy actually come in contact with something containing MDMA in the past?

The edge of the curtain pulled back and the gray-haired man in an equally festive Christmas hat crouched down to the child's level. "Who's your friend, Matty?"

"A police dog named Liberty," Matty replied cheerfully. "She's on duty so you can't pet her."

The man's eyebrows rose and faint worry flickered in his eyes. He ran both hands down his jeans and stuck out his right one. She took his hand and shook it.

"Hi, I'm Matty's grandfather, Fred Jolly," he said. He nodded to a smiling woman with long white braids who he'd been setting up the stage with. "That's my wife, Irene."

"Nice to meet you," Noelle said. "I'm Officer Noelle Orton and this is my partner, Liberty."

"Are you two looking for something?" he asked.

"We are," Noelle confirmed, hoping the couple would respect it if she left it at that. So far the NYPD had chosen not to go to the public with news about the trace drugs found at the dock, as details were still scarce and they didn't want to start a panic. "You guys are handing out toys at five?"

"Hopefully," Fred said. "We had a bigger turn out than expected at a previous event this morning and had to send someone to get more toys from our warehouse."

"Where was that event?" she asked. Could that have been where little Matty came into contact with whatever scent Liberty had picked up on?

"A fire hall in Queens," Irene called, as she walked over to join them. "You should talk to our son, Adam. He runs our family charity and he's down at the loading dock, waiting for the van."

She gestured toward an unmarked double door behind the stage. Yeah, judging by the tug on the leash, Liberty thought she should go that way too.

"Thanks," Noelle said. "Will do."

She followed Liberty across the floor, through the door, and out into a dingy back hallway as she radioed Raymond and filled him in. Raymond reported back that he and Abby hadn't found anything at the toy store. She thanked God another store's inventory had checked out clean. Liberty's pace quickened until she was practically running down the hall. They pushed through another door and out into the cold. The sky was gray with thick clouds that blocked out any glimmer of the setting sun. Flakes pelted down from above. The loading dock was empty except for a white van with *Jolly Family Charity* on the side. Liberty pulled her toward it. Then the dog stopped outside the van's back door and barked. Could this be the lead they'd been waiting for?

"Morrow," Noelle spoke into her radio. "Liberty's reacted to the Jolly Family Charity van."

"Gotcha," Raymond's voice came back. "Stay with the van. I'll speak to the Jollys and get their permission to search it."

"Understood," Noelle said.

Liberty whimpered loudly. Noelle ran her hand over the back of her partner's head to reassure her.

"I hear you," Noelle said. "There's something important in that van. But we can't just open the door and check it out without permission or a warrant, unless we hear someone in imminent danger inside."

A motor rumbled and the van lurched forward, as if someone behind the wheel had just mashed their foot on the accelerator. Liberty barked furiously as if to say, *it's getting away!*

"The van's pulling out!" she shouted to Raymond and reeled off the license plate as the van sped away. *Help me, Lord!* Even with traffic, there was no way she'd catch up to it on foot.

A black four-door pickup tore around the side of the building. She ran toward it and raised her badge. It screeched to a halt.

"Stop!" Noelle called. "NYPD! I need to commandeer your vehicle!"

The passenger door swung open and she looked up into the sharp blue eyes of the man in military fatigues from the poster.

Was this Adam Jolly?

"To chase my stolen van?" he asked.

"Yeah," she said.

"Get in," he said. "I'm driving."

Adam's right hand tightened on the steering wheel, letting his injured left hand with its three missing fingers stay down by his side. His van had just left the lot with his wounded and kidnapped employee, Quentin Stacy, trapped in the back. As long as Quentin's phone stayed on and was sending out a signal, Adam's phone would be able to track his GPS. But pausing to wait to pick up a passenger hadn't been part of the plan and he didn't have a moment to waste.

"I drove tactical convoys in Afghanistan," he said, "I was a corporal in the United States Army. I've got a man inside the van and a way to track it. Now come on."

She quickly checked in with someone named Morrow on the other end of her radio, then glanced at her dog. "Liberty, back seat."

The Labrador leaped in the passenger door and climbed in the back, pushing its furry body through the gap between the seats. Half a second later and the cop was in with her seat belt buckled and the door closed.

"You sure you want to bring a dog on a high-speed chase?" he asked.

"She's my K-9 partner," the cop said, "and considering New York traffic, I'll be impressed if you actually manage to speed."

He chuckled. Okay, so the cop was decisive and seemed to have a sense of humor. He cast her a quick side glance as he put the truck into Drive. She was beautiful too,

Adam thought. Unusually so, with high cheekbones and long dark hair tied tight in a bun by the nape of her neck.

"Noelle Orton," she said, as if sensing his glance. "Brooklyn K-9 Unit."

"Adam Jolly," he said. His eyes cut to the windshield. "Nice to meet you."

He peeled out of the lot, glancing from the road ahead to the blue dot on the map on his cell phone mounted to the dashboard.

"Nice to meet you too," Noelle said. "What do you mean, you have a man inside the van?"

He pulled his truck out onto the street. Traffic surrounded them almost immediately, and the van was nowhere in sight. But the tiny blue dot showed the van had turned left. He followed.

"I got a call from my employee, Quentin Stacy," he added. The light ahead turned yellow and a car coming the opposite way was trying to push a left turn. He gritted his teeth, pressed the gas and steered around it. The car honked loudly, but he'd safely made the light. "He was in the back of the van about to unload toys when a masked man caught him by surprise and stabbed him. Thankfully, he managed to call me."

"So it's a kidnapping?" Noelle pressed. "Or the masked man panicked and left with him in the back?"

Good question.

"I don't know," Adam admitted. All he knew was that he was not about to let him die. He'd lost more people than he liked to count, from those he'd served with to Matty's mother. The last convoy Adam had driven overseas might've ended in an IED explosion that had cost him a few fingers and prematurely ended his military career. But others in his armored vehicle had lost their lives.

By the look of things, the blue dot was heading toward the parkway. If he was right, maybe he could cut them off, or at least catch up. An alley loomed ahead on his right. It hadn't been plowed, but there was only a couple feet of snow on the ground. He shifted into four-wheel drive and prayed his hunch was right.

"And you're tracking him on GPS?" she asked.

"Yup." He swerved down the alley. The ground was slick with slush beneath his tires. His wipers beat hard and fast against the falling snow like a metronome. Noelle turned to her shoulder radio and filled Morrow in on the pursuit, reeling off details about his van, their route, and the likely route of the vehicle they were after with a precision and sharpness that impressed him. He left the alley, merged with traffic, glanced at the rearview mirror and caught sight of a blond furry face. It looked like Liberty was smiling at him.

"Oh, so you think this is fun, do you?" he asked.

Noelle turned to him and he realized she'd ended the call. "Are you talking to my dog?"

"Maybe." He realized he was grinning. Not that there was anything really to smile about, but Noelle had that same quality of lightening the tension while still keeping focus that some of the best soldiers he'd served with had. "You've called for backup."

"Police and paramedics," she said. "They'll try to cut him off."

The Belt Parkway on-ramp loomed ahead. He took it and a sudden prayer of thanksgiving filled his lungs—the shortcut had worked and he could see his van just a few vehicles ahead. It was also speeding and driving recklessly by the looks of it. But he had eyes on it and it sounded like help was on the way.

Thank you, Lord. Please, help the paramedics get to Quentin in time.

Okay, now it was just a matter of keeping eyes on the van. Traffic was heavy enough that people would probably complain, but light enough some people were still trying to speed. He watched as the van dodged left and right, swerving between vehicles without signaling. He gritted his teeth, set his jaw and followed.

And now that he was no longer watching both the dot and the road, he realized there was something he hadn't even asked. "If you didn't know about Quentin, why did you even want to chase my van?"

She prayed under her breath and decided to trust him.

"We have reason to believe illegal drugs might've been smuggled into the country via the port in a shipment of toys," she said. "We were doing a search of the mall and your family pointed me in the direction of the loading bay. Thankfully, the toys in the mall store seemed to be clean, but Liberty smelled something in the van. But before I could investigate further, the van took off."

She'd met his family? He wasn't sure why that thought struck his mind as hard as it did, but he didn't have time to figure it out. Because the van cut a hard left, coming too close in front of a slow-moving truck. The truck swerved, hitting its brakes. But it was too late. As he watched, the truck jackknifed, smashing into the van as it did so and taking out another car in its wake. The car right ahead of Adam braked hard and swerved, fishtailing out of control. He heard the sound of horns blaring and the screech of another vehicle smashing into the guardrail to his left.

A multi-vehicle accident was happening and they were caught right in the middle.

"Hang on!" Adam shouted. Gripping the steering wheel tightly, he fixed his eyes on the road ahead and prayed. "Lord, keep us and everyone else on this road safe!"

Then it was like time slowed, as it always had when he'd found himself maneuvering under fire in a danger zone. He set his sights on the safest route he could find and drove, blocking out the noise and steering around the crashing cars and chaos as it spiraled out around them. A small blue car spun out in front of him. Noelle gasped sharply. He weaved between the accidents and heard his own taillight crack as a car skidded into them from behind, knocking them forward.

But he slid his pickup past the jackknifed truck, pulled to the verge and braked. Only then did he let himself breathe and take in the wider scene around him. The accident was behind him now and clear road lay ahead. He looked up at the sky and thanked God, half expecting to see the hot searing blue of the Middle East horizon instead of the dark gray of twilight in New York.

"Thank you," Noelle said. Her fingers brushed his right arm, which was still locked in a tight grip on the steering wheel. "That was incredible driving and you might've just saved my life."

She shoved the door open, and cold air rushed in. He felt Liberty's soft snout brush against his cheek and he couldn't tell if it was the dog's way of thanking him or making sure he was still breathing. A man in dark clothes and a ski mask bolted past them down the verge. Noelle jumped out, shouting for Liberty even as the dog leaped to her side. Cop and dog bolted after the man. For a second he could see Noelle yelling into her radio for backup, then they disappeared from view. But for a moment he just sat there, with one hand on the wheel, the other at his side, and his heart beating so hard it felt like it was trying to ricochet its way out of his chest. He prayed and thanked God. Then he pelted across the pavement in the opposite direction toward his van. The front door lay open, and the driver was gone. He ran to the back and yanked it open.

Bashed and dented toys littered the floor, their brightly colored wrapping paper ripped and tattered. For a moment he couldn't see Quentin. Then he heard a groan and saw something move under a pile of boxes to his right.

"Quentin!" Adam dropped to his knees. "Don't move. I'll get you out."

He pushed the gift-wrapped toys aside. There lay Quentin, a former military veteran himself almost two decades older than Adam. His face was pale. Blood seeped through the sleeve of his ski jacket. Instinctively, Adam pressed one gloved hand against the wound to staunch the bleeding. With the other he checked the man's pulse. Thankfully, it was strong.

Quentin's eyes fluttered open. "Adam?"

"I'm here," he said. "Just hang on. Ambulances are on their way. Are you okay? What happened?"

Already he could hear the sirens coming.

"He offered me five hundred dollars." Quentin's voice was so quiet Adam could barely hear it. "All I had to do was let him take the truck and walk away... I said no."

Adam's chest tightened. When Quentin had left the military, he'd had a hard time adjusting back into civilian life. He'd served time for drug possession with intent to sell and was currently on parole. Adam couldn't imagine the strength it had taken for him to turn down that kind of money.

Probably not even a fraction of the drugs' worth, if the cop was right.

"Who was he?" Adam asked.

"Dunno," Quentin said. "Big man, ski mask, heavy Eastern European accent that seemed fake."

The door behind Adam flew open, then paramedics were asking him to step aside as they reached for Quentin, helped him carefully onto a stretcher, and carried him out and into the ambulance. Adam looked around at the wreckage of damaged gifts that he, Quentin and his family had so carefully and lovingly wrapped. His heart was so heavy he didn't even know what to think. Then he felt the van shake as two more bodies leaped up into the back and a gentle hand brushed his shoulder.

"Adam?" Noelle's voice was surprisingly tender. He turned and looked up into her deep green eyes, the color of fir trees and pine. Worry pooled in their depths. "Are you okay?"

He glanced down and realized his gloves were streaked with Quentin's blood. He pulled them off.

"Yeah." He stretched and stood. "According to Quentin, a masked man offered him five hundred dollars to walk away and let him steal the van."

If Noelle was surprised by that, it didn't show in her face.

"And you believe him?" she asked.

"Yes," Adam said, "of course. I saw you chasing someone. Did you catch the guy?"

"No." She frowned. "He got away. But

police, paramedics and firefighters have arrived. It'll be a little while before they clear all the vehicles and get us moving again. But, thankfully, despite some injuries, there seem to be no fatalities." He thought she was about to say something more, but instead she stopped and looked down at the dog as if Liberty had just spoken in a frequency only Noelle could hear. "Search."

The dog's ears perked. Liberty pressed her body through the packages, furrowed out a large red box, dropped it at Noelle's feet and barked.

She'd found something.

TWO

The dog's bark was triumphant. Noelle's heart leaped in her throat. She glanced from her K-9 partner to Adam, and then down at the large shiny red gift on her feet.

"Go ahead and open it," Adam said. "I'm not about to demand you get a search warrant."

She would've chuckled if she'd been able to breathe. Noelle knelt down, tightened her gloves and slowly unwrapped the present. A large toy dog with bright eyes looked out at her from the clear window of a box. It was a black lab, by the looks of it, and was about sixteen inches tall with a big green-and-red bow around its neck.

"It's a FlupperPup," Adam said.

So said the large swirly letters on the box. But that didn't mean anything to her. She turned the box over in her hands. A squad of eight dogs was listed on the back. "Never heard of it."

"It's the must-have toy this year," Adam continued. "They're like little furry robots that can respond to voice commands, follow you around and learn tricks. They connect to the internet and have some kind of camera too. Apparently, some breeds are rarer than others. We've managed to receive a few to give out at events."

"And where do you get your toys from?" she asked.

"Large companies mostly," Adam said. "We do get individual donations and some schools and churches do toy drives. But the bulk of what we give away comes from large organizations. Our suppliers are pretty generous."

"And how many toy suppliers do you have?" she asked.

"Eighteen," he said. "And before you ask, we pulled these toys from our warehouse. There's no way of tracking who donated any given toy."

She opened the top of the box carefully and pulled the dog out. The toy was surprisingly sturdy and incredibly fluffy.

"My son Matthias... Matty...really wants one for Christmas," Adam added.

She thought of the boy with the mop of dark curls, eager smile and blue eyes the same color as his daddy's.

"Did you get him one?" she asked.

"Not yet," Adam said. "They're pretty pricey."

She turned it over in her hands.

"Presumably, there are some pretty heavy robotics, a camera and computer inside," she said. "But I don't see a hatch. How do you put the batteries in?"

"No batteries," he said. "Seems those days when toys all ran on big fat Cs or Ds like when we were kids are long gone. You plug it into the wall to charge and it connects to the computer via WiFi."

Well, this one no doubt had a hatch. Liberty's tail was still thumping and that was good enough for her. She pulled a knife from her pocket, opened the blade and slit it into the toy's soft fake black fur. She peeled the fur back. Sure enough there was a large cavity inside. But instead of the expected electronics, there sat a large baggie filled with thousands of brightly colored pills shaped like white snowmen, green Christmas trees and red bells. Liberty barked triumphantly. Noelle sat back on her heels and blew out a long breath. She guessed it was two to three hundred thousand dollars' worth of MDMA—probably a strain of Ecstasy.

"They look just like candy," Adam said, as if reading her mind.

They did. The thought of a child stumbling upon a bag of colored drug pills on Christmas morning and mistaking them for candy sent chills through her.

She radioed the Brooklyn K-9 Unit and filled them in on what she'd found. Thankfully, several officers were already on their way, including Raymond and Abby. She watched as Adam's hand reached out as if wanting to pat Liberty, then caught himself before he did just as little Matty had.

She told Liberty to keep searching. Adam closed his eyes and his lips moved in what she guessed was silent prayer. She looked away to give him privacy.

"Your van will be towed back to the station so the forensics team can go over it," she said when he opened his eyes. "And they'll also get a warrant to check your warehouse."

He bristled. "Except I've got a couple hundred kids expecting Christmas presents."

"I know," she said, "and I'm sorry, but we can't risk drugs falling into the hands of children."

"Of course we can't." Adam sounded almost offended. "But toys can be checked before we distribute them. We can't let these kids go without toys at Christmas. For a lot of them, this could be the only real present they get this year."

She felt her eyes widen. Did he think she didn't know that? Or that she didn't care?

"Trust me, I'm not in the business of stealing toys from children at Christmastime," she said. "But we've got a lot of ground to cover and a lot of warehouses to search. We've already cleared several so far."

"But surely there's something you can do," Adam started.

"Like what?" Noelle asked. "I can explain your situation to my boss, but even if you're leapfrogged to the top of the list, I can't guarantee your toys will be released until after Christmas. And I can't let you take these toys. You're making it sound like you think I'm heartless for doing my job."

He blinked, like he hadn't been expecting pushback. Well, he may have done an incredible job pursuing the stolen van, that didn't mean she was about to let him run the show. "That wasn't my intention."

"Trust me, I feel terrible about this," she said, "and I'm sorry if it makes you think less of me. Hopefully you can have both the toys in the truck and the warehouse back in a few days."

"Tomorrow is Christmas Eve," Adam said. "I don't have a few days. I have kids waiting for toys as we speak, plus a brunch at a community center tomorrow and then another giveaway tomorrow evening."

Her heart ached for him, for his family and the children too. But there was only so much she could do.

For a moment she thought he was about to argue. But all he said was, "I need to get back to my family."

Sirens filled the air and lights flashed outside the door. Even more backup had arrived.

"Again, I'm really sorry," she said, "and I am really thankful for your help. Someone will be in touch."

She slid her gloves off, stuck them in her pocket and reached out her hands toward him before her brain fully realized what she'd done. She'd almost tried to hug him. Instead, Adam reached out with both hands and took hers in a double handclasp.

"It was nice to meet you, Officer," he said.

The two-handed handshake was awkward and seemed to be lasting longer than it should. She looked down and startled to realize the three middle fingers were missing on his left hand. Injury, she imagined.

She looked up into his blue eyes. "It was nice to meet you too, Corporal. And if I don't see you again, Merry Christmas."

Adam drove back to the mall as quickly as he safely could. His heart felt like it was thudding through his chest and he didn't quite understand why. Between the multi-car accident, Quentin's injury, the candy-like Ecstasy pills inside the toy dog and the children back at the mall awaiting toys, he had so much to think and pray about. But somehow the one single thing that was floating front and center in his mind was the face of Officer Noelle Orton.

Had she thought he was rude when he'd pressed her on whether she really needed to impound his van and warehouse? And if so, why did that thought bother him so much?

There was something about her that rattled him in a way he couldn't explain and didn't know how to shake. There was just something, a quality, that got to him. She was beautiful, sure. But more than that, she was professional, focused and driven, and while he was beside himself with worry about what he was going to do, somehow he also admired the way she'd dug her heels in and stood up to him.

He couldn't remember ever being this impacted by a woman before. Matty's mother, Carissa, had been his best friend since kindergarten. They'd known each other for years before he'd even once thought of kissing her. She'd been his sweet, steady and reliable confidante for over twenty years when she'd died of breast cancer, leaving him with their toddler son and a broken heart. The incredible and life-changing love he'd felt for Carissa had been completely different from the sudden jolt to the system meeting Noelle had been.

So, what was it about Noelle that he couldn't shake? The intensity in her eyes? The way her chin had risen when she'd stared him down? The slight flicker of surprise that had brushed her gaze when she'd noticed his injured fingers as she'd held his hands? In the relatively short time they'd spent together, she'd never noticed his injury. Then when she had, she'd taken it in stride.

He pulled into the mall's back lot, ran up the loading dock and pushed through into the hallway where he found his father waiting for him.

"Everything all right?" Fred asked. "And if not, what can I do?"

That was his dad in a nutshell. The toys were missing, the event was supposed to start any minute and Adam had disappeared for over half an hour without explanation, but all his father was focused on were solutions. Adam was beyond grateful.

"Quentin was threatened at knife point by a thief who stole our van," Adam said. He kept walking and his dad matched his pace. "He was injured, but he's okay and in the hospital. Unfortunately, the police found drugs stashed in one of the toys, impounded the van and locked down our warehouse."

He heard his father thank God that Quentin was safe and pray for his healing.

"Is that what the K-9 officer was looking for?" his dad asked. "Nicole?"

"Noelle," Adam corrected. What an appropriate name that was for a Christmas case. The veteran in him appreciated Liberty's name too. "And yes. Although the mall store was clear, somehow a toy dog stuffed with drugs got mixed up in one of our toy shipments. So, until the Brooklyn K-9 Unit sorts out how, we've got no toys."

They reached the double doors and pushed through them back into the mall. The sound of hundreds of excited children and their parents filled his ears.

His heart sunk. *Lord, help us out of this mess!*

"Daddy!" Matty ran toward him, with his grandmother, Irene, one step behind him. "I met a yellow police dog with a special black smudgy ear!"

"Hey, little man!" Adam bent down and scooped his son up into his arms. "Her name is Liberty, right? So did I!"

"I wanted to pet her but I didn't," Matty said. "Because she was working."

"I wanted to pet Liberty too," Adam admitted. He hugged his son, as his father quickly and quietly filled his mother in. He watched as a prayer crossed her lips. He echoed her silent prayer with one of his own and set his son down. "I'm going to call all of our suppliers. Hopefully one of them will come through with replacement toys."

"In the meantime, your mother, Matty and I will lead everyone in some Christmas carols," Fred said. "Unless, you'd like to do the music while I make the calls?"

"No, thank you," Adam clasped a hand on his father's shoulder. "You guys have got this."

As a teenager it'd been all but impossible to pry him away from the guitar. For now, it was still on the list of things he had to reteach himself after the accident.

Not five minutes later, he was pacing the floor behind the stage, praying under his breath and juggling both his and his parents' cell phones as he placed calls from all three at once, thankful his mom hadn't misplaced hers again, as she so often did. He left messages, called second and third times, and tried personal cell phone numbers—anything he could do to get toys for the kids. No one was answering. In one ear, he could hear his dad strumming, his mom and Matty leading the crowd in carols. In the other ear, he could hear the cell phones ringing.

Help me, Lord. I don't know what to do.

His phone clicked.

"Adam? It's Lou Shmit, owner of Dotty's Toys."

"Lou, hi!" Adam nearly dropped the phone as he fumbled to snap it to his ear.

"Got a message from you," Lou said. "So did my secretary and warehouse guy. Your toys were stolen?"

"Something like that," Adam said. He wasn't sure if he'd put it exactly like that but he'd left so many messages it was hard to keep track, and he imagined Noelle would want him to keep the news that drugs had been found in one of his toys close to his chest. "I'm standing in a shopping mall right now, with a couple hundred kids and no toys. Then we've got a morning event tomorrow and another tomorrow night."

There was a pause on the other end. Then he heard Lou blow out a long breath and Adam felt his heart sink.

"I'm sorry," Lou said. "We had the Brooklyn K-9 Unit searching this place this morning thanks to some big smuggling case. I don't know the details, but rumor is they're apparently checking everyone who got a toy shipment in through the port this month. Figured to let them in right away and not wait for a warrant. But it tied up our warehouse and guys for most of the day before we were finally cleared and our trucks went out late. I'll see if I can do something for tomorrow but I'm not promising anything."

"Got it." Adam's phone beeped that another call was coming in. "Sorry, I've got to quickly take a call. Can you hold?"

"Sure thing," Lou said.

Adam clicked through to the other line. "Hello?"

"Mr. Jolly?" The voice was female and crisp. "My name is Gillian Nicks. I work for Ace Distributors."

"Hi, yes, and call me Adam." He'd placed a couple of messages for his regular contact at Ace, but he'd never dealt with Gillian. However, they were also the farthest away. Even if they had spare toys, it would take hours to reach them. "How can I help you?"

"Actually, I'm calling to see how I can help you," Gillian said. "I understand you're currently at a toy giveaway without toys. Can you give me the details?"

"Sure," he said and rattled them off quickly. "Can I put you on hold? I have another call on the line."

"I'll call you back," she said.

Now what had that been about? He ended the call and clicked back to Lou. "Hey, sorry about that."

"I've got some partially good news," Lou said. "We can get toys for both your events tomorrow. We just can't do anything about today."

"Tomorrow is better than never," Adam said. It wasn't everything he needed but it was a start. "I owe you one."

A burst of cheers, followed by applause rose from the crowd of kids on the other side of the stage. What was happening? He ended the call and went to look. Two uniformed teenage employees from the large toy store at the end of the mall were pushing a shopping cart overflowing with toys toward them. Two more followed, carrying armfuls of stuffed animals. Before he could figure out the reason for the parade of approaching toys, his phone rang again. "Hello?"

"Adam, it's Gillian again from Ace," she said. "I've spoken to the manager at one of our retail partners and they've agreed to meet the immediate need for toys for your event. Apparently, I'm to tell you the Brooklyn K-9 Unit searched their store and stockroom this afternoon and found no problems. They should be bringing toys to you now."

Relief flooded over him so suddenly his knees buckled.

"Thank you, God," a prayer slipped out under his breath.

"Now, it'll just be back-room stock," Gillian added, quickly, "and on the condition my company provides an overnight restock before the store opens tomorrow. They'll probably be posting about this on their website to maximize positive publicity and might ask your charity for comment and pictures. Also, I can't promise it'll be high-end toys or that they'll be wrapped."

"But they'll be toys for the kids," Adam said, "and that's all that matters."

His heart swelled with joy. The cheers rose louder as the store's teenage clerks began piling presents under the tree. Matty was bouncing so high on the balls of his feet he was nearly levitating.

"I have to go," Adam said. He had to coordinate the giveaway and explain to his baffled parents what was going on. "I really can't... I can't thank you enough..."

Gillian chuckled softly.

"You're welcome," she said. "My sister goes to the same church as a journalist named Sasha Eastman, whose fiancé is with the Brooklyn K-9 Unit. Apparently, an Officer Noelle Orton of that precinct put out an emergency prayer bulletin on the church's site about your charity being in urgent need of toys and Sasha posted it on her social media. When I saw it, I recognized your name and tried to see what I could do."

He had Noelle to thank for all this?

He didn't have time to even begin to think about what that meant. For the next two and a half hours, his hands, heart and mind were full with distributing toys to smiling children. And despite the added complications, not a single child left disappointed and without a toy. For that he was beyond happy and thankful. The event had finished, store fronts were being shuttered and Adam was sitting on the stage with Matty half asleep in his arms, when he looked up to see a familiar face and her canine partner walking through the mall toward him.

"How did it go?" Noelle asked.

"Better than I thought it would," Adam admitted. "One of our distributors got the mall toy store to pitch in and help us out. I'm told that's thanks to something you posted online?"

Noelle pressed her lips together and nodded slightly. "Well, I'm not totally heartless."

A deep and unexpected chuckle bubbled up from somewhere deep inside his chest.

"I never said you were," he said. "But if you're here for a toy, I'm afraid you're too late."

She shook her head. "No, I'm here because of a larger, and potentially pretty serious, situation I'd like to talk to you about. I have to go back to the station now. But is there somewhere private we can meet up later tonight and talk?"

THREE

Two hours later, Adam paced the living room of his family's home in Bensonhurst and fought the urge to keep looking out the window. The mall had been closing when Noelle and Liberty had arrived and Matty had been exhausted, so Adam had suggested she come by the house later. Noelle had been quick to agree, saying she'd drop by when she got off duty. Now, for some reason, he was as anxious as a kid waiting for Christmas morning. Did he secretly miss the adrenaline of serving on the battlefield? Or was it something more than that?

Lord, what am I feeling? And, more importantly, what do You think I should do about it?

There was a knock at the door. He looked up to see a police SUV impressively parallel parked in a tight spot on the street outside the house. He walked to the door with his heart beating so hard he almost worried she'd be able to hear it. He opened the door and there she stood on his front doorstep, with a smile on her face that seemed to light up the corner of her eyes. His mouth went dry. "Hey."

"Hey, Adam," Noelle said. She'd swapped her police blues for a soft red sweater, black leather jacket and blue jeans. Her long dark hair fell loose around her shoulders. And for a long moment he just stood there, feeling himself grin. Then he felt a nudge against his leg and looked down. Liberty was out of her K-9 harness too and wagging her tail at him.

"Come in," Adam said, "please." He stepped back and made space as Noelle and Liberty walked through the doorway. Noelle took off her boots and Liberty shook off the snow. "Let me take your coat."

"Thank you." Noelle turned and shrugged her coat off into his hands.

The soft, sweet smell of her filled his senses.

"Liberty's here! Liberty's here!" Matty charged around the corner, screeched to a stop and looked from Liberty to Noelle and back. "Liberty's not in uniform. Does that mean I can pet her?"

"Yes." The smile on Noelle's lips grew wider. "Liberty is off duty and pettable."

"Yay!" Matty knelt down, threw his arms around the canine and hugged her, burying his face in her fur. Liberty gave the boy a lick and something about the dog's eyes made Adam think Liberty was laughing. Then Matty sat back and looked up at Noelle. "Why does she have a smudgy black ear?"

"I don't know," Noelle said. "But it's very rare and special." Then she leaned down toward the boy and whispered loudly, "In fact, Liberty is so special that one time some very bad guys wanted to stop her from doing her job so she had to go into hiding!"

"Whoa!" The little boy's eyes grew wide. "Like witness protection for dogs?"

Noelle nodded conspiratorially. "Yup, but she's safe now."

Matty's smile doubled in size and something twinkled in his eyes.

"Was it woof-ness paw-tection?" he asked.

Noelle tossed her head back and laughed. It was a beautiful sound and tugged at more threads inside his heart that he could count.

"Come on, Liberty!" Matty darted down the hall. "Let's go."

Noelle glanced at Liberty and nodded. The dog followed the small boy down the hall, and Noelle turned to Adam.

"I haven't seen Liberty this happy in months," Noelle said and her eyes shone. "What happened with those 'bad guys' I just mentioned was that a gunrunner put a pretty big bounty on her head last year, and we had to stop taking high visibility cases for months. It was unbelievably hard for her. She loves working so much and she was really frustrated. It was hard because

I couldn't explain to her why she was suddenly benched."

"I can only imagine," Adam said. He turned as his parents came out of the kitchen to greet Noelle.

He'd intentionally kept the information he'd told his parents about the situation vague. But now she filled them in, quickly and simply, on how a baggie full of smuggled Ecstasy pills had been found inside a toy dog. Liberty hadn't reacted to any other of the toys inside the van, and so far the narcotics team hadn't found anything at the Jollys' warehouses or offices. Quentin was in stable condition, despite needing forty stitches, and had been questioned briefly and would be interviewed at length tomorrow. Something about the way Noelle mentioned Quentin's name made him suspect that she thought his employee was hiding something.

But it wasn't until his parents had excused themselves and they were sitting alone in his living room that she volunteered what had been on her mind.

"Did you know Quentin Stacy has a criminal record for drug possession with intent to sell?" she asked. "And that he's on probation?"

"I did," Adam admitted. "The way he tells it, he got addicted to painkillers, forged prescriptions to get ahold of more pills and then started selling them. I'm not excusing his past, but he had a rough time readjusting to civilian life from the military and made some pretty big mistakes. Thankfully, he got his life back on track."

"And you believe his version of what happened?" Noelle asked.

"I do."

She didn't say anything for a long moment. Instead, they sat and listened to the sound of snow buffeting against the window and Matty's excited voice coming down the hall as he showed Liberty around his room. Adam expected her to press him about Quentin again. Instead, her gaze fell on the guitar beside the couch. "You play?" she asked.

"Used to," he said. "Haven't gotten around

to relearning it after the accident. The convoy I was driving in Afghanistan hit an IED at the side of the road. I only lost a few fingers and ended up with a medical discharge. But a lot of really good men lost their lives."

"I'm sorry," Noelle said. "That's hard."

There was both a simplicity and sincerity to her tone that he appreciated.

"I keep meaning to pick it back up and teach myself how to play again," he said. "I used to lead all the carols at my parents' giveaway events."

"You're an only child right?" she said. "No brothers or sisters?"

"Yup," he said. "Just me."

"Same here." She smiled and he wasn't sure if she was interviewing him or trying to get to know him better. "Did you grow up in this house?"

"No," he said. "My parents had a house in New Jersey. Carissa and I bought a tiny place in Queens when we got married." He paused. "Carissa was my wife, and my best friend, and Matty's mother. We lost her to breast cancer three years ago."

"I'm really sorry for your loss," Noelle said, "and for Matty's."

Her hand brushed his arm sympathetically and then his fingers of his injured hand linked with hers in a quick and supportive squeeze. Then he pulled back and leaned his elbows on his knees.

"Thanks." Just thinking of Carissa made whatever he felt for Noelle all the more ridiculous. He liked Noelle. He liked her a lot. But he'd known his late wife for fifteen years before he'd even felt the slightest twinge of anything romantic for her. "When she died, I sold the apartment, my parents sold their house and we bought this place in Bensonhurst together. Matty lived here with them while I was deployed."

"Your son's amazing," she said.

"He is," Adam said. There was another pause, longer this time, and he was surprised they'd lasted this long without Matty charging in. Then again, he seemed pretty taken with Liberty. "You said you wanted my help with something?"

"I do," Noelle said. He watched as she took a deep breath and emotion flickered across her face. But when her eyes met his, they were strong and steady. "Canadian organized crime is one of the biggest suppliers of MDMA and our intel indicates drug smugglers have been bringing it into the country via the ports. We're talking large quantities here. The empty shipping container, which started this investigation, probably contained thousands of items stuffed with pills—in this case, toys. Whoever the buyer is who received it, they're a new player we haven't dealt with before, and they probably have hundreds or thousands more hidden somewhere, which will then be passed on to distributors who'll fan out and sell it across the country. Nobody out there is smuggling just one single baggie of pills through the ports this way."

Right, this wasn't a social visit. This was her job and he'd do well to remember that. He sat back.

"And obviously, the K-9-team who searched my family charity didn't find thousands of toys filled with drugs in my warehouse," he said.

"Right." She nodded. "Also, they're not just looking for a big warehouse of items, they're looking for an infrastructure and contact network used to distribute the drugs. It'll be a huge operation."

Not a small mom-and-pop-style charity, then.

"So how do you think the toy got in my van?" Adam asked. "Do you think it was planted?"

"I don't know what to think," Noelle said. "But Liberty initially seemed to pick up a slight trace of something around the stage at the mall, specifically around Matty. Now, it was so faint she disregarded it almost immediately. Sometimes K-9 dogs double check an area before moving on, especially if there had been something there at one point that's now gone. She also could have been leading me to the shipment of toys in the van. But it's also possible Matty somehow inadvertently came in contact with another toy containing pills at some point and that's what she was detecting."

Adam let out a long breath. He ran his hand over his mouth.

"Matty hasn't been in the warehouse for weeks and the only person who packed the van was Quentin," Adam said. "I don't want to scare or worry Matty by making him think something's wrong, but the idea of him accidentally coming into contact with MDMA is worse."

"I know," Noelle said. "Normally I wouldn't even mention it to you, let alone pursue it. But even though we don't know each other well, it's so obvious to me how much you love your son and want to protect him. I knew that you'd want to know."

He swallowed hard, not sure what was caught in his throat. She was right. While his rational brain told him there was probably no reason to worry, just the idea of Matty coming near those kinds of drugs was unthinkable. "So, what do I do?" he asked.

"I want to run something past you," Noelle said. She leaned forward. "Liberty and I are off duty, but being a highly trained K-9 dog, Liberty will still signal a little if she detects narcotics or firearms. She instinctively flinches. My colleague Officer Raymond Morrow says his K-9 dog, Abby, *dances* a little when someone who's carrying drugs passes by her on the street, or in a coffee shop or office. Liberty just gets a little extra alert. If you and Matty give us a tour of the house, and Liberty signals to something, we can then pursue a proper search. If not, then at least you'll have peace of mind."

"We can do that," he said. "I have a licensed handgun in a safe in my room and my father was on prescription painkillers for his back last year, but I'm pretty sure there's nothing like that here now. Thank you both for telling me Liberty might've sensed something around Matty and offering to help put my mind at ease by making sure whatever it was isn't in the house. You said there was a second thing?"

"The Brooklyn K-9 Unit will be sending officers to monitor the two toy giveaway events you're doing tomorrow," she said. Yeah, he'd expected as much. "Seeing as it's Christmas Eve and it's the last two big giveaway things you're doing this year, if someone is using your events to move drug-laced toys, they've got a pretty tight window to do it in. It was really clear from talking earlier just how much helping those kids matters to you. And we don't have to be disruptive or wreck what you're trying to do to be effective at our jobs. So, I just wanted to let you know we were open to finding ways to help accomplish your goals while fulfilling ours."

He sat back. Whoa. Not only had Noelle taken him aback by her thoughtfulness about Matty, she'd now done it twice. He'd learned firsthand while deployed in Afghanistan how hard it was to juggle being compassionate to those around him while also doing his job at the top of his game. The fact she was even aware of how uniformed cops could impact attendees at an event like his impressed him more than she knew.

"I appreciate this so much," he said. "But I like the idea of having you visible and in uniform. I think it'll be good for the kids to see cops helping out at something like this."

She smiled. "I agree."

The floor creaked with the telltale sound that Matty was coming down the hall, followed closely by the clack of Liberty's paws. A moment later his son's smiling face appeared around the corner.

"Can I help with your police work?" Matty asked. "I'm good at noticing things. And Liberty and I make a good team."

Noelle slipped off the couch and crouched down at his level.

"Well," she said. "I'm wondering if you know anything about FlupperPups."

Matty's eyes widened. "I do!"

His son turned and ran down the hallway before Adam could remind him to walk. Seconds later he was back holding a department store Christmas flyer. Matty pointed at the row of FlupperPups that matched those she'd seen on the box. There were eight breeds, including a beagle, a golden Lab and a husky that had been enthusiastically circled. But it was the small word typed under the black Lab dog with the big red bow that caught his eye: *Rare.* He glanced at Noelle and could tell she'd caught it too.

"What does it mean this black dog is rare?" Noelle asked, and he suspected it was because she wanted to hear Matty's take.

"It means it's supposed to be special because it's hard to find," Matty said. He pointed his finger down the line of dogs. "They go really-easy-to-find, sort-of-easy-to-find, harder-to-find and super-hard-to-find. But it's silly. Why does being hard to find mean it's better?"

Adam noticed the husky that Matty had circled was right in the middle of the list.

"I agree," Noelle said. "Making toys hard to get is very silly."

Matty beamed. Soon afterward, Adam gave Noelle and Liberty a tour of the house.

To his surprise, and with his permission, Noelle turned it into a game, getting Matty to help hide a special small rubber ball in different rooms. Sure enough, Liberty twitched her ears near his bedroom safe, but beyond that the dog didn't react to anything else in the house. He was relieved. An hour later, after several games of hiding the ball and a quick mug of hot chocolate with both large and mini marshmallows with his parents and Matty, Noelle and Liberty started their goodbyes. Adam got Noelle's coat and held it for her while she slid her arms into her sleeves. After a few more last-minute goodbyes from Matty to Liberty, Adam walked Noelle out.

They stood outside for a moment, in the darkness, with snow falling so faint around them it was almost invisible except when it crossed the golden shafts of streetlights. His eyes searched her face.

"You're worried," he said.

"I am." She looked up into his eyes, and for the first time since they'd met, it was like he could fully see through her crisp and impressive professionalism to the vulnerable person inside. "Is it that obvious?"

"I don't think so," he said. He wasn't sure how he could tell. "But it just seems that something's bugging you. Do you want to talk about it?"

His hand brushed her shoulder and she didn't step away from his touch.

"You saw those pills," she said. "They look exactly like candy. There could be thousands of toys stuffed with drugs out there. According to our forensics team, the contents of that baggie alone was worth over two hundred thousand dollars on the street. People have been killed for less. Your family could be right in the middle of this and your toy giveaway was almost completely derailed."

"But it wasn't in the end," he said. "Every kid went home happy today, I'll protect my family and you'll solve this case. It'll be okay. I have faith. And you should too."

Then somehow he found his arms parting. She stepped into them, and he hugged her to his chest. She wrapped her arms around him and hugged him back. The strong, driven, beautiful cop he'd only met a few hours earlier stood there, in his arms, as if it were the most natural thing in the world and he'd been hugging her goodbye outside his front door for years.

"Noelle!" His mother's voice sounded behind him. He and Noelle sprung apart as his mom ran down the front steps. She'd come out in such a hurry her coat wasn't done up and she was wearing his father's shoes instead of pausing long enough to put on her own boots that required lacing. "I just remembered something."

Heat rose to Noelle's face as Irene hurried down the narrow driveway. What must she have looked like standing there with Adam's arms around her? She glanced at Adam, but he wasn't meeting her eyes. Irene hurried to her car and popped the trunk.

"I'm sorry. I completely forgot I had this," Irene said. She leaned in, lifted a blanket and pulled out a FlupperPup. It was a husky just like the one Matty had circled. "I bought it for Matty yesterday and hid it in the trunk so he wouldn't see me bring it in."

But Noelle knew from the moment she took it that it didn't have drugs inside. The weight and balance were entirely different, and when she shook it lightly, nothing rattled. She held it up to Liberty and the dog agreed. No drugs. Irene was worried that she'd wasted Noelle and Liberty's time. But Noelle was quick to reassure her that it was actually really helpful to know what a FlupperPup that wasn't filled with drugs felt like. Not to mention, she was thankful for the well-timed interruption of the awkwardly long and probably ill-advised hug. She wasn't even sure what it was about the handsome widowed father and military veteran with the deep compassionate heart and impressive precision-driving skills that affected her quite the way it did. But whatever it was, she made sure that her good-night and goodbye were extremely professional.

Despite the fact that Noelle tossed and turned so much in her bed that night that

Liberty went to sleep on her dog bed, No-elle was laser-focused on keeping everything highly professional when she greeted Adam and his family the next morning at the community drop-in center. No more hugs. But she needn't have worried, because Adam's crisp handshake and polite "Good morning, Officer," made her suspect he regretted the hug too.

Thankfully, there was plenty of work to do and no opportunity for any more time alone or awkward moments. The event was in a large community shelter and included a free brunch, carol singing and games. Both she and Liberty, and Raymond and Abby, had done a complete sweep of the place before it had opened. Then the shipment of toys had been searched and sniffed thoroughly by the dogs when they'd been delivered, before they were placed under the tree. But they'd found absolutely nothing suspicious.

Raymond and Abby relocated to the front door once the event started, taking occasional strolls around the room. At his suggestion, she and Liberty stayed close to the Jollys, helping as they handed out toys, led everyone in carols and dished out food for the potluck. By midmorning she was standing beside Fred, helping him serve up bagels and toast at one end of the long buffet line, with Liberty lying under the table by her feet. Adam was partway down with Matty, singing carols together as they served up bacon and sausage. Seeing how happy they were together made her own heart swell. She knew she wasn't supposed to get emotionally attached to people on her cases. But she couldn't help but admit she liked the Jollys.

Especially Adam. He was this amazing mass of contradictions. Incredibly focused one moment and yet flexible the next. Professional in an instant and yet deeply caring. There was just something special about him, like an Advent calendar with so many doors she had yet to see inside. His eyes met hers above Matty's head, and even though she knew she should look away, she found herself holding his blue-eyed gaze.

Help me, Lord. I like this man a lot more than I should.

A soft wet snout brushed her hand. She looked down. Liberty was at her feet and looking up at her, her deep brown eyes warm and insistent. Had she sensed Noelle's discomfort?

"I'm going to take Liberty for a quick walk around the building," she said, turning to Fred. "Can you handle the toast until I get back?"

"Sure can." Fred chuckled. "But if something goes terribly wrong I'm sure it won't be long until somebody steps in to save me."

Noelle laughed. "Thank you. Back in a minute."

She nodded to Raymond and his K-9, Abby, across the room and signaled that she was going to walk around. He nodded. She looped Liberty's leash around her hand and slipped out from behind the table. Out of the corner of her eye, she could see Adam's eyebrow rise in question as he watched her go. She led Liberty through the tables of happy families eating brunch and past the towering tree decked out in sparkling lights, and then led her down the back hallway toward the alley behind the center. The noise of the celebration faded. She heard Liberty bark softly and felt her tug her leash.

She radioed Raymond. "I'm walking toward the back entrance, and Liberty's signaling me that she smells something."

"In this area it could be a small-time drug deal or someone smoking up," Raymond's voice came back. "Abby's paws were dancing like crazy outside earlier. Could be something, could be nothing. Stay safe and keep me posted."

"Will do," Noelle said. She looked down at Liberty. "Let's go, Liberty. Show me."

The dog's ears perked, her nose started to twitch and her pace quickened. Okay, she definitely smelled something. Noelle followed her down the hall, through a back door and out into the snow. Pale gray sky stretched above her. A van with a Dotty's Toys logo on it was parked in the alley, its white sides streaked gray with slush and dirty snow. It was smaller than the one they'd unloaded from earlier and she didn't know Dotty's was sending a second batch of toys. Was it for the next event? She signaled the dog to slow and started toward it, keeping one hand tight on the leash and the other ready at her weapon. Something thumped inside the back of the van.

"Police," she called. "Is everything okay?"

The van's back door flew open. Gift-wrapped toys tumbled out onto the ground. A man in a black ski mask launched himself at her.

FOUR

Where had Noelle gone? The question rattled around in the back of Adam's mind as he dished bacon and sausage up onto people's plates and listened to Matty chatting cheerfully in his ear. Noelle's colleague Officer Morrow hadn't budged from his position by the front door, so wherever Noelle had gone, everything was probably fine. And yet Adam couldn't shake the feeling something was wrong.

Maybe he'd seemed rude when he'd stuck her down at the other end of the buffet table with his dad. But for some reason, being up close with her rattled something within him like loose screws inside his internal engine. He hadn't been able to get her out of his head once since the moment they'd met. If he'd been a lot younger and a whole lot more foolish, he might have blamed his heart and said he'd fallen head over heels into something. But he'd never believed in so-called "love at first sight," almost hearing the air quotes in his head as the phrase crossed his mind. His attraction to Matty's mom had built incredibly slowly into something deep and long-lasting. And nothing like this jittery feeling inside him.

But, besides all that, he'd also never been one to ignore his inner danger alarm when it was going off. And right now, that was sounding too.

He gestured to his dad.

"Where'd Noelle go?" he called, forcing his voice to stay upbeat and light.

"For a walk," Fred said with a smile.

Okay, but what kind of walk? The kind when your legs just need stretching or when something is wrong?

He glanced at his mom. "You and Matty got things covered here for a minute?"

Worry flickered in his mom's perceptive eyes but her face flashed a smile that he suspected matched his. "Sure. Not a problem."

And if there was a problem, it wasn't his to solve, he reminded himself as he grabbed his jacket from behind the table, shoved his arms through and headed down the hall in the direction Noelle had gone. They weren't colleagues or serving in the same unit. Yet for some reason, his pace quickened as he pushed through a door to his left. Immediately, bracing cold wind and thick flakes assailed him. The sound of a struggle came from somewhere to his right along with the noise of Liberty barking. He ran toward it, saw a white van ahead of him, and then he saw Noelle, down on the ground, fighting with a male figure in blue jeans, heavy boots and a black ski mask.

The figure had a gun.

Prayers shot like flares through Adam's core.

"Hey!" he shouted. "Leave her alone! Let her go! Now!"

And maybe it was a silly thing to shout at a masked man attacking a cop, but he hadn't really been thinking. The man looked up, distracted. Noelle delivered a sharp elbow to his jaw that sent him falling back. His gun slipped from his grasp.

"You're under arrest!" Noelle shouted as she leaped to her feet.

But it was too late, as the man turned and ran, pelting down the narrow alley, with what looked like a large box jammed into his jacket. Noelle ran after him with Liberty by her side, shouting into her radio for Officer Morrow, giving him a rundown of what had happened and details of the direction the man was going.

Adam found himself running after them, through the narrow space between dingy brick buildings, being careful to keep far enough back to stay out of the way.

A fence rose ahead with a large lock wrapped around the gate. The masked man jumped up and scaled it.

Noelle glanced back for a fleeting moment.

"Adam!" Noelle shouted, and only then

did he really know that she knew he'd been following her. "Stay with Liberty!"

"Got it!" he called.

Noelle scaled the fence, climbed over it and tumbled down the other side. Adam felt something brush his leg, glanced down and saw Noelle's K-9 partner looking up at him under shaggy eyebrows. Liberty whimpered slightly as if the dog could read his mind and felt the same urge he did to run after Noelle and help her. No matter how skilled Liberty was at detection, it wasn't her role to chase criminals down like some other K-9 breeds. It wasn't Adam's job either.

Instead, all they could both do was watch as Noelle chased after the man. He slipped and she leaped, tackling him from behind and bringing him down into the snow. A gift-wrapped package fell from his jacket as she cuffed him and read him his rights. Officer Morrow and his K-9, Abby, ran down the alley from the other direction and helped haul the cuffed man to his feet. Noelle walked over to the gate, unlocked it and signaled to Liberty. Then she knelt down and offered the dog the gift-wrapped package. There, between the gaps in the torn wrapping paper, Adam could see it was another black FlupperPup. Liberty's back tensed and her ears perked as she sniffed it. Then she barked.

"More drugs?" Adam asked.

"Looks like it," Noelle said.

She met his gaze and held it. What did she think of the fact he'd come looking for her and run after her?

"Hey, Adam! Adam!" A male voice yanked his attention past her. "Tell them you know me! And that I'm a good guy!"

Adam felt his jaw gape. The person shouting to him for backup was the same masked man who'd just been holding a gun to Noelle. His mask had been pulled up and now Adam could see his face. He was in his late twenties, with the sallow skin of someone who'd taken too many illegal substances and tried and failed more than once to claw his way back from that life. He turned away from the man, not wanting to interfere and Noelle matched his stance.

She bent her head toward Adam's. "You know who he is?"

"His name is Olly Whit," Adam said softly. "My family and I volunteer at the community meal here twice a month. He comes in sometimes with his daughter."

"I didn't mean any trouble!" Olly was yelling loudly now, seemingly to anyone who would listen. "My little girl's mom won't let me see her or bring her today. And I needed a present for her for Christmas."

Adam felt the pressure of Noelle's gaze searching his face. "Is that true?" she asked.

"I think so," Adam said. "Or close enough. He has a little girl. She's about three or four. He's often losing visitation rights. He does have a record for theft and drug use, but from what I know, it's low-level stuff."

Noelle pulled a knife from her pocket and slid it first into the box and then the FlupperPup. It was faster and more precise this time now that she knew how to open it up.

"Well," she said as she held up the dog for Adam to see. "He was carrying a toy filled with drugs."

Sergeant Gavin Sutherland, head of the Brooklyn K-9 Unit, cut a tall and imposing figure, coupled with the kind understanding for the hard work his team did that made Noelle determined not to let him down. Especially since 'Sarge' had come to the community shelter personally to brief her on the status of the drug case.

It had been almost an hour since Olly Whit had been carted off in handcuffs. The community event had now ended, people had filed off home and the center had closed its doors. Noelle and Liberty stood beside Sarge in the alley behind the center, sheltered from the snow by an overhang.

"What's your read on Olly Whit?" Sarge asked.

"He's a low-level weed dealer," Noelle said. "No indication he's dealt in MDMA, Ecstasy or anything like that. And nothing that would indicate a connection with a larger criminal enterprise. His story of stealing a FlupperPup for his daughter is plausible."

She was pretty sure she wasn't telling Sarge anything he didn't already know, but that he was looking for her take on it. Despite the years she'd spent as a K-9 trainer and thanks to the length of time she and Liberty had been forced to take off from high-visibility cases due to the bounty on Liberty's head, when it came to being a K-9 officer, she was still very much a rookie.

"So, you believe him?" Sarge asked.

"It would be premature to judge his credibility until he's been interrogated," she said, feeling her chin rise. "Again, he has a record of minor offenses but nothing of the scale of what we're looking for. Officer Morrow told me that the community center manager confirmed Whit was kicked off the premises for being drunk last week and suspended from attending events here for the next thirty days. Whit says he came by, hoping he'd be able to talk his way in, saw the truck and decided to go for a quick grab-and-dash instead."

"And he just happened to grab the only toy in the truck that was full of drugs?" Sarge pressed.

Was he testing her? Or was she just tired? Or both? She hadn't exactly slept the night before and had been working as much overtime as she could get her hands on.

"He grabbed the only FlupperPup," she said. "Certain FlupperPup breeds are rarer than others, making them the most valuable. The black dog with the red bow is the rarest of the dogs. It's hardly uncommon for rare toys to get stolen and resold on the streets at Christmastime. It's possible he was covering his bases by picking something he knew he could resell to some desperate parent for some quick cash."

Matty's voice crossed her mind, reminding her it was stupid to judge how special a toy was based on how hard it was to find. Adam had taken the little boy with the bright inquisitive eyes and infectious smile home, along with Fred and Irene, while she'd been coordinating things with Raymond. Thankfully, the fact Whit had run from the scene meant the arrest had taken place away from the center and not disrupted the event.

Once the drugs had been found, she and Adam had barely exchanged more than a quick wave goodbye before he'd jogged back to the center. She hadn't known what to think when Adam had run after her when she chased after Olly. But it had felt instinctive and almost comforting to have him there. And, of course, she was thankful he'd identified her suspect.

"Lou Shmit, the owner of Dotty's Toy's, says he has no idea how one of his vans showed up here after the event had already started." Sarge's voice dragged her attention back to the matter at hand. "He says there appears to have been a mix-up in his warehouse, after someone called claiming to be from the center, reporting they'd run out of toys. Also, no idea how a drug-filled dog showed up in his vehicle, considering K-9 officers swept his entire warehouse yesterday. He claims he's being set up and someone used his van as a cover. Now his business is being searched by police again, wrecking their ability to meet the shipments they wanted to get out before Christmas. They're practically on lockdown. He's hopping mad about it."

He continued giving her a quick rundown of the larger operation. There were officers tracking the distribution angle and investigating several different gangs, interviewing Olly Whit, Quentin Stacy and Lou Shmit's warehouse team, as well as continuing to search toy stores and warehouses for the remaining FlupperPups. Not a bad reminder that no matter how much pressure she put on herself to work all the hours, she and Liberty were still just a single cog in a larger machine.

A yawn escaped Noelle's lips. She quickly ran her hand over her mouth, hoping to hide it. But she could tell by the way Sarge's eyebrows quirked that he'd seen it. He glanced at his watch.

"Your shift ended twenty minutes ago,"

he said. "Go clock out, then go home and get some rest. If anything major happens, someone will contact you."

"Actually, I put in a request for overtime," she said. "There's another Jolly Family Charity toy giveaway tonight and I'd like to be there. I've been on this lead ever since it broke and have been building a connection with the Jolly family. I might catch something other officers don't."

"I know, and you applied for overtime tomorrow too," Sarge said. "I'm denying your request for today and only granting you a partial shift for tomorrow morning."

She felt herself frown.

"I get that you and Liberty felt sidelined for a very long time," he added, "through no fault of your own. I appreciate your dedication and everything you bring to the team, but you can't make up for missing months of high-profile fieldwork by working yourself to exhaustion now." His voice was firm, but there was kindness in his smile. "The NYPD has been cutting back on officer overtime hours for a reason. You and Liberty are a terrific team. We need you at the top of your game. You won't be that without sleep."

Then his eyes flitted over her shoulder and widened slightly.

"Then again, if this is a personal thing, you can always attend the event off duty," he added.

She turned and followed his gaze. There stood Adam, on the sidewalk behind them, close enough to be waiting but far enough away to not be listening in. Her breath caught in her throat. He was so impossibly handsome, with his strong jaw, broad shoulders and caring eyes. Couple that with his deep heart for his family and dedication to serving both his country and those in need, Adam was probably the most extraordinary man she'd ever met.

He was the kind of man she'd never expected to look her way, let alone have her back.

"Sergeant Gavin Sutherland," Sarge said, as he strode toward Adam with his gloved hand extended to shake the other man's hand. "You must be Corporal Jolly."

"Call me Adam," he said. He shifted a reusable shopping bag full of Christmas gifts from one shoulder to the other, then reached out his hand and shook Sarge's firmly. "Pleasure to meet you."

"Likewise," Sarge said. "I'm afraid I don't have much of an update on the situation, but I'm happy to answer any questions you might have."

"Thank you," Adam said. "I appreciate that." Then his eyes flitted to Noelle. "Actually, I was about to run an errand and wondered if Noelle and Liberty were up to joining me for a walk."

At the word *walk*, Liberty's ears perked. She glanced up at Noelle as if asking, *Please, can we?* Noelle bit back a chuckle.

"Actually, I need to go back to the station to clock out of my shift," Noelle said.

"Which I can handle for you," Sarge said quickly. "Go for your walk now. Unwind, stretch your legs and then pop back into the station when you can. I'll sort your shift log. No problem. You've been working way too hard and could use a break."

What was Sarge doing? His words, tone and bearing were every bit as professional and direct as usual. But there was a faint tinge of something almost brotherly to his voice. Then she watched as Sarge's grin spread and felt her face flush. Her boss seemed to be under the mistaken impression that Adam was asking her out on a date. Which it couldn't be, right? Adam's only interest in her was in connection to the drugs case, right? Yet, as Adam said goodbye to Sarge and then turned to her and smiled, something warmed inside her chest.

She told Sarge she'd see him later, looped her hand through Liberty's leash and turned to Adam. "Let's go."

Adam led the way and she fell in step beside him, as they walked side by side through the snowy city streets, feeling every bit as comfortable to have him there on one side as it did to have Liberty on the other. Lampposts festooned with sparkling red-and-green wreaths rose ahead of them out of the snow. The brightly decorated windows of barbershops, diners, stores and bodegas on both sides wished them a Merry Christmas. Small talk flowed easily between her and Adam as they walked. There was just something so comfortable about being around him. He was somehow like an old friend she hadn't seen in years, but also sort of like a book she was engrossed in from the first page. They'd already walked three blocks before she realized she hadn't asked him where they were going. What's more, somehow she wasn't in a hurry to. There was just something nice about simply walking side by side through the falling snow.

"How did you end up having two such different careers?" she asked. "What's the connection between driving a military convoy in Afghanistan and giving out toys to children at Christmas?"

He chuckled. It was warm, deep and the kind of laugh that seemed to pull her in closer.

"The connection is my heart," he said. He ran his hand over the back of his neck, then shivered as if melted snow had slipped down his collar. "It's like my heart has two separate but connected sides. Joining the military to serve my country was a calling. It beat inside my chest like a drum, telling me that it was what I was meant to be doing with my life. But the connection to my family was just as strong, in a quieter and softer way, and I love being part of the charity my parents built. I loved serving my country one hundred percent, and yet I also wake up one hundred percent happy and thankful for the work I do now."

"My parents believe really strongly in the value of hard work," Noelle said. "They instilled in me a strong sense of responsibility and dedication to my job. They always tell me not to come home for the holidays, or summer, because those are the best times of year to get overtime. They're great people, but they don't have that relaxed sense of joy that your folks do."

Adam stopped in front of a squat brick walk-up. She did too. He frowned.

"I asked my parents to stay home with Matty tonight instead of coming to the final giveaway," he said. "With everything that's happened, it just felt safest. Matty tried to be brave, but I could tell he was really disappointed."

It was definitely the smart move to make considering there'd been an incident right outside the last event. Still, as she watched Adam's shoulders droop, she could feel her own heart sink.

"For what it's worth, I think you made the right call," she said. "But I'm sure that doesn't make disappointing Matty any easier. I'm not working tonight, but Liberty and I can be there as friends if you need backup."

She stepped toward him and the space between them shrank as her free hand brushed his shoulder. Liberty's head butted her knee and the dog whined softly, as if she sensed the people were sad and wished she could help.

"Thank you," Adam said. "It would honestly be great to have you there."

He shifted slightly and her hand slid off his shoulder. But instead of stepping back, he moved closer and his fingers brushed hers, linking their hands for one long moment. Then he pulled away and turned toward an apartment building. He shifted the bag higher on his shoulder.

"Come on," he said. "I've got some presents to drop off."

She followed him up the steps, saw him hesitate at the broken keypad and then push the door open. They stepped into the building and immediately Liberty tensed slightly. Noelle looked around but saw nothing but a door to the left that read Employees Only and a bank of key-scarred mailboxes to her right. Whoever had been carrying drugs through here earlier was now gone. She ran her hand over the back of Liberty's neck, just behind her black-smudged ear, to reassure the dog.

She followed Adam up the stairs. "I completely neglected to ask where we're going."

Oddly enough, she'd been so happy and relaxed just enjoying Adam's company somehow the question had completely skipped her mind.

"We're here to drop some gifts off for Olly Whit's daughter and her mom, Lonnie," Adam said. "They're unlikely to have much, especially with him in jail over the holidays, and I wanted to make sure they were taken care of."

Something swelled in Noelle's chest and she found herself thanking God for this incredible man with such a deeply caring heart.

They reached the third floor and walked down a hallway that smelled of cooked meat, marinara sauce and the sickly sweetness of whatever had been last tossed down the garbage chute. Adam knocked on a door with what looked liked a child-made pompom Christmas wreath on it. The woman who opened the door was thin and looked barely more than twenty, with long blond hair streaked with blue. A little girl peeked out from behind the multi-colored couch behind her. Noelle glanced down at Liberty. The dog's body was relaxed and her tail was wagging. It seemed she didn't detect anything from Lonnie or her apartment, and Noelle thanked God for that.

Lonnie glanced from Adam to Noelle and Liberty, but when Adam reassured her that Noelle was just there as his friend, she relaxed slightly. Lonnie smiled as Adam handed her the bag of gifts for her and her daughter, and when Adam encouraged her to come to the next free community meal, she said she'd try to make it.

"It would be great to see you both there," Adam said. "And if you ever want to talk to anyone about Olly or anything else, I'm here. You can trust Noelle too."

Lonnie's lower lip quivered.

"Olly's a good man," Lonnie said. "He just makes bad decisions. But he's not a bad person."

"I know," Adam said. "I think most people are good at heart, but some make bad choices and some are also given a bad deal in life. People are complicated." Lonnie nodded. Adam's smile was kind and warm. "Merry Christmas! Hope to see you again soon."

They left and walked back down the hall and they started down the stairs.

"I hope you don't mind I didn't try to ask her any questions or invite myself in," Adam started.

"No, judging by how tense she was when you first showed up, my guess is she wouldn't have been comfortable with that," she said. "It's really important not to scare off potential witnesses, especially as I'm off duty and someone else will have interviewed her." Their footsteps reached the second floor. "Honestly, I was just thinking how really, really nice it was of you to do that. But why did you invite me along?"

"Because I know that even if she does know something, she won't sell out Olly to the police," Adam said. "My impression has always been that Olly knows he's too toxic for his wife, but also doesn't want his daughter growing up with her father in jail. But I thought if I vouched for you personally, and introduced you as a friend, she might be more willing to trust you if she did know something."

They kept walking down the stairs and Noelle found herself praying for Lonnie and her daughter, and everyone else whose lives had been touched by drug smuggling. She prayed for the officers fanned out across the city trying to solve the case, and finally for the incredible man now walking beside her and his family.

Please, Lord, bring this case to a close soon, before anyone else gets hurt.

The sound of gunfire shook the air, echoing up from the floor beneath them. It was like someone was firing wildly up the center of the stairwell toward them.

As fast as her instincts were, Adam's were even faster.

"Get down!" Adam's voice thundered in her ear as he threw his arms around her, pulled both her and Liberty down into the corner of the stairwell and sheltered them with his body, as bullets ricocheted around them.

FIVE

Adam felt his arms tighten around Noelle and her head tucked into the crook of his neck, as they crouched together on the floor. His heart pounded in his chest. Prayers poured through him. Then the sound of gunfire stopped, silence fell and they pulled away from each other. For a moment their faces were so close that if one of them had flinched even a little their lips would've met in a kiss. Instead, she jumped up and ran down the stairs, calling for backup on her radio, Liberty by her side.

He rocked back on his heels and gasped a breath, as the realization of what had just happened swept over him. His instinct had been to protect her. He hadn't thought about himself or keeping himself safe from danger, just like he hadn't when he'd chased after her through the alley.

No, when he'd heard the sound of gunfire, all he'd wanted to do was keep Noelle safe. The need to protect her had been overwhelming, then relief had engulfed him when he'd realized she was okay, followed by an odd sort of loss when she'd run down the stairs without him.

Help me, Lord. It's like everything I feel when I'm around this woman is so much louder and stronger than regular feelings that it's deafening.

He gasped another breath, pushed to his feet and ran down the stairs to the lobby. He couldn't have been more than a few flights of stairs behind her and yet it was like arriving into an entirely new world. Two young men in blue jeans and hoodies stood talking with a gray-haired man, who seemed to be the building manager. Within moments two cops had run through the door, who he guessed must've been patrolling the area nearby, followed shortly afterward by more police in a flurry of sirens.

And there was Noelle in the middle of it all, managing the scene, calming the witnesses and briefing the officers as they arrived. Even off duty, there was something commanding about her. Adam stayed for a while, long enough to give a statement to one officer and double check that Lonnie and her daughter were okay. But once again, Noelle was so caught up in talking to the police, making calls and just being her incredible, professional and impressive self, that he found himself hovering on the edges of the scene for a while, watching her and wrestling with his own confusing heart.

He told her that he was heading home unless she needed him to stick around to give her a ride. She thanked him but said she'd be fine. Then he walked back to his vehicle alone and drove home, feeling his thoughts chase after him like buzzing drones that had locked onto something deep inside him. Noelle didn't need him. He wasn't her colleague, they weren't serving in the same unit and he definitely wasn't her bodyguard. Sure, she was investigating a case that had to do with his family's charity, but that was where their relationship ended.

So, why did he feel so happy and complete when he was near her? And like something crucial was missing when she wasn't there? Why did it feel like she'd leaped into his heart and taken it over, just like she'd tried to commandeer his truck the day before? Had he gotten bored with his civilian life? Had he gotten too complacent about reteaching himself the skills he'd lost when he'd been injured? Did he miss the adrenaline rush of risking his life to save others?

Guide me, Lord. I'm all questions and no answers. Help me be who You've made me to be.

One of the most important reminders of who God had made Adam to be was waiting for him in the window when he got home. He waved to Matty, then got out and jogged toward the house.

"Hey, Matty!" Adam called as he opened the door. "The snow's really soft and squishy right now. Want to come help me build a snowman?"

"Yes!" Matty yelped, running so quickly to throw his coat and boots on, he almost slipped in excitement. A smile filled Matty's face and lifted Adam's heart.

Thank you, Lord, for all You've given me.

The next couple of hours passed quickly and happily, as he and Matty packed and rolled snowballs together and sang Christmas carols at the top of their lungs. What had started as one snowman grew into an entire snow family, with a snow dad, snow son and two snow grandparents, by the time he heard footsteps crunch the snow behind them. He turned to see Noelle and Liberty standing in the driveway. Noelle was back in civilian clothes, dressed in blue jeans, boots and a bright red coat that matched the giant bow on Liberty's collar.

She waved hello. "Hey, guys! Those are some good-looking snowmen."

"Hey," Adam said, his mouth feeling oddly dry.

"Hi, Noelle!" Matty chirped. He bounced

on the balls of his feet like he wanted to run toward them but was waiting for permission. "Liberty's off duty, right?"

Noelle laughed. It was a beautiful sound. "Yes, Liberty's off duty. We both are."

She leaned down and whispered something in Liberty's ear, then she dropped the leash and the dog practically galloped across the snow toward Matty, stopping just short of barreling into the boy. Matty threw his arms around Liberty and the dog's tail thumped in the snow.

Adam met Noelle halfway up the driveway and their hands hovered in the air for a moment as if they both wanted to hug but weren't sure if they should. They ended up shaking hands, awkwardly, then crossing their arms and turning toward Matty and Liberty as the boy and dog tussled in the snow.

"The suspect was apprehended three blocks from the shooting," Noelle said. "He was eighteen and says his drug dealer gave him the gun and told him he'd give him a thousand dollars to follow me and shoot. I was the target. Not you or Lonnie."

As glad as he was to hear that Lonnie and her daughter hadn't been targeted, knowing that Noelle had been in danger didn't make him feel any better.

"He panicked and just shot up the stairs, hoping he'd hit something," she went on with a shrug. "He was just a kid. Police picked up his dealer too, who says word on the street is that some new big player on the drug scene has got some really potent MDMA pills to sell and they're shopping them around to various dealers. Rumor was that a deal was taking place at the community center. Seems he spotted me at the center, heard I'd intercepted the drop and figured scaring me off the case might give them an edge with the new player."

Adam felt a chill spread down his spine. And was surprised when she just sighed.

"Of course, Olly is sticking by his story of just grabbing the wrong toy," Noelle added.

"Tell me someone is looking into this

new player angle," Adam said. Not that he doubted for a moment someone would be, but more like he needed the reassurance of hearing her say it.

"A whole team of people are on it," Noelle said. "Some of the best cops I know are questioning every single person involved and digging into each of their stories. This is a sprawling investigation. As far as we can tell, it was a crime of opportunity by one dealer hoping to earn cred with this new player in the drug game, and not a larger threat against me. Thankfully, Lonnie and her child are fine. A colleague got them a place in a really nice women's shelter. It's like a bed-and-breakfast with lots of other kids."

"And we don't have any idea why this new player would use my gift-giving event as a cover to do business," Adam said.

"That's what everyone's trying very hard to find out," Noelle said. "Do you recognize these men?"

She held up her phone and showed him pictures of both the teenager who'd fired the gun and his dealer, which he guessed had been taken around the time they'd been questioned. Adam didn't recognize either of them. Noelle didn't seem surprised, especially if she was right that they were low-level dealers who just happened to see her at the community center.

"So, what do we do now?" he asked.

"We go to your event," Noelle said, "we give out toys and we're thankful there's a large police presence there. I was thinking we could go together and take your vehicle, since mine's a police SUV."

"Sounds good."

They headed into the house, taking Liberty and Matty with them, luring the latter with hot chocolate and cookies.

"Come on, Liberty," Matty called, as he stepped through the door and shook off his boots. "You can help pick up the crumbs!"

Irene ushered Noelle toward the inviting warmth and smells of fresh baked goodies in the kitchen. Adam walked to his large bedroom at the end of the hallway. He'd of course offered his parents the expansive master bedroom when they'd first bought the house, but Fred and Irene had chosen a large room in the finished basement with an en suite bathroom. He changed into fresh clothes, a Christmas sweater and perched his silly hat with the jangly bells on his head.

Then he sat on the edge of his bed and prayed. He wished he could talk to Carissa. She'd always been the steady rock he could rely on to center him when he felt tossed in the storm. He knew what she'd say. She'd say the exact same thing he'd written to her in the letter he'd left her to read if he died overseas on the battlefield. He'd written he didn't want her to be alone forever, but to find a husband who was worthy of her love and who'd be a good daddy to Matty. But how was he supposed to know how he felt? His love for Carissa had grown slowly and gently for years. Whatever it was he felt for Noelle had completely broadsided him.

He followed the sound of chatter and laughter back to the kitchen. It seemed Matty had given Noelle his silly hat for the night and she was trying to figure out how to fit it on her head.

"Adam!" His mother's voice rose as she turned to him. "Tell Noelle that she's coming for dinner either Christmas Eve or Christmas itself."

Noelle laughed and turned to Adam. "As I already told your mother, I'm working."

"Both Christmas morning and Christmas night?" Irene said. "Who does that? Work one and come here for food the other."

Irene crossed her arms as if the matter was settled. But as Noelle laughed again, she didn't seem the slightest bit cowed, let alone persuaded. And he wasn't about to get in between the two strongest women he knew. He chuckled, popped one cookie in his mouth and palmed three more for the road. There was a smattering of good-byes, hugs and final pats for Liberty. Irene pushed a napkin full of even more cookies into Noelle's hands. Then a few minutes later, they were in his truck, heading to the final giveaway event.

"Thank you for sharing your family with

me," Noelle said, as he drove through the snowy streets. "They're really wonderful."

"I hope my mom wasn't too pushy," Adam said. "She's always been rounding up people and inviting them over, for Christmas, Easter and the Fourth of July. My friends used to call her Mrs. Jolly Holiday."

Noelle didn't answer for a long moment and he wondered if he'd said something wrong. Liberty leaned forward from the back seat and stuck her head between the seats. Noelle scratched it thoughtfully.

"My parents are amazing, but they've never really liked Christmas," Noelle said. "My dad has never been good at emotions. He was really focused on being a good provider and making sure my mom and I never went without, so he tended to take all the overtime he could. Dad was the only son in a big family and money was tight growing up. My mom has always been twitchy and uncomfortable about the holidays. She never talks about her childhood, but I know it was rough and I always got the impression Christmas brought up bad memories.

They always made sure I had presents and a tree. But I could tell they were doing it to make me happy."

She drew her arm back and rested it on the center console. Liberty leaned forward and set her snout on it.

"Christmas is hard for a lot of people," Adam said. "Some are on a tight budget or work in essential services and can't take a day off. Some are bereaved, or their family lives far away. The pressure the media puts on the holiday doesn't help."

"No, it sure doesn't," she agreed.

"There's no one right way to celebrate Christmas," he went on, "and I like to think that what we do helps take a bit of the pressure off."

She nodded for a long moment. Then ran her other hand over Liberty's head.

"My parents send me gifts," she said, eventually, "and I send them a care package too. They were proud of me when I told them I'd be working through Christmas. I knew that's what my dad would say—take all the available hours, show them you're a team player, especially since you gave up so much for…"

Her voice faltered. His hands tightened on the steering wheel.

"For what?" he asked.

"For Liberty," she said. "I was a K-9 trainer for a long time, but I'm still a rookie when it comes to being an officer. My parents weren't big fans of my making the switch to begin with. Their attitude was pretty much—why take the risk of a job change when things are going so well in what you're already doing? Liberty and I had only been partnered a short while when a gunrunner put a bounty on her head for being too good at detecting smuggled weapons. My parents didn't understand why I agreed to stop taking high-profile cases and didn't just ask to switch to another dog. But I was so blessed to have Liberty as my partner I couldn't just ditch her because it got hard." Adam pulled to a stop at a red light, reached over and brushed her fingertips with his.

"Love and loyalty are complicated things," she added.

"Yeah," he said. "They are."

They reached the center where the final event was being held. He parked the truck and they went inside. Uniformed NYPD officers greeted them at the door and he could see others inside, including several K-9 teams, but the increased police presence hadn't dampened the crowd of eager children and parents. Lou Shmit from Dotty's Toys had called as the giveaway was wrapping up to ask how things had gone. Adam thanked him again and told him everything was great. Yet somehow, even though the event went off without a hitch or even a hint of trouble, and every child left with a smiling face and a Christmas gift, something sat heavy in his heart. And whatever the weight was, it grew even more as the night ended, the doors closed and he drove back home.

They drove in awkward silence through the dark and snowy streets, no easy small talk that had flowed between them earlier.

The snow had grown heavier now, clogging up the roads, snarling traffic and reducing the stop-and-go pace to a virtual standstill in places. Why did his heart feel so unbelievably heavy? The final gift-giving event of the season was over. Maybe so was his role in the case Noelle and her colleagues were investigating.

"You can drop us off here," Noelle said. He glanced to his right and saw her police vehicle parked up ahead. "I'm guessing Matty will be in bed by now."

She was right and if Matty woke up and found Noelle and Liberty there, it would take him ages to go back to sleep. He pulled over to the curb and turned to Noelle, wishing they could go somewhere private and talk. He couldn't just say goodbye and let Noelle disappear from his life.

But what exactly was he supposed to do? What was he supposed to say? How could he possibly explain he didn't want her to leave his life but also didn't think he was ready for a relationship yet? How did a man ask a woman like Noelle to just hang out with him and let him get to know her better while he figured out his heart? She was worth more than that.

"So, you'll get in touch and let me know what happens with the case?" he asked, his words feeling clunky as they fell off his tongue.

"Someone definitely will," Noelle said.

She flashed him a dazzling smile and a slight panic crossed his heart to realize this might be the last time he'd ever see it.

Help me, Lord. I have to do something. I have to say something. What's wrong with me? Why is this so hard?

She reached over to hug him goodbye. His arms slipped around her. Her cheek brushed against his.

"Thanks for everything, Adam." Her voice was low in his ear. "Merry Christmas."

"Merry Christmas." He turned his head toward hers.

Then it happened. Their lips brushed. Had she kissed him? Had he kissed her? Had it been an accident? He had no idea.

All he knew was his arms were around her and that somehow he was kissing her, and she was kissing him. She pulled back; so did he. They blinked at each other and he couldn't tell if the kiss had lasted a minute, seconds or barely an instant.

His phone rang in his pocket. He pulled it out and saw it was home.

"Hello?" he answered.

"Daddy?"

His son's voice sounded panicked, scared and like he was fighting back tears. Fear pierced Adam's spine.

"Matty? Are you okay? Where's Grandma and Grandpa?"

"Bad men broke into the house." Matty choked back a sob. "And I'm hiding."

In an instant Noelle had dispatch on the phone, reeling off information as she dashed to her vehicle long enough to grab her weapon, even though she was off duty and would have to stand down unless she was intervening to immediately save a life. The moment she leaped back into the truck,

Adam gunned the engine and raced to his house. He'd wedged his cell phone into his scarf to create a makeshift hands-free device and filled her in as he drove, Noelle passing the information on to dispatch. Matty had woken up, found the living room empty and gone downstairs to his grandparents' basement suite. Then he'd heard *banging* and *loud and angry* men shouting, so he'd dashed into the laundry room and crawled into the bundle of sleeping bags, patio cushions and summer picnic blankets Irene kept in the very bottom of the linen closet to hide. Noelle's heart ached to think about how frightened the little boy must be.

She glanced at Adam and told him the response time that the dispatcher had given her. "Seven minutes."

His face paled. The lights were out at the Jolly family's house. Adam pulled past it and into an empty driveway one door down.

"The neighbors are away for Christmas," Adam explained, as he cut the engine. "I have permission to be on their property and promised to shovel their sidewalk. Figured parking here, instead of my own driveway, would keep the perps from realizing we're here."

"Smart," she said. She couldn't imagine how the focused military combat veteran and panicked father sides of him were battling inside his heart right now. "Police are on their way."

And an estimated seven minutes out thanks to the snow and traffic. How long and achingly scary could that be for Matty who, judging by the time of the call, had already been hiding in the closet for almost five minutes?

The festive hat Matty had lent her was sitting on the back seat. She stuffed it into her pocket in case she needed it to get Liberty to trace his scent.

"Police are on their way, Matty," Adam said into the phone, pressing it against his ear as he ran up the neighbor's driveway. "Stay there, stay safe and they'll find you very soon." Noelle watched as he swallowed hard. "And Grandpa and Grandma too. I promise."

Adam must've put the call on speakerphone, because as she and Liberty reached his side, she heard Matty's voice, soft and terrified. "Daddy, be fast."

"I will. I promise. I love you," Adam said. "Now the call might get quiet, but I can still hear you, okay? And if you talk to me, I'll answer."

She watched as he put the call on mute, she guessed to keep Matty from hearing anything that might scare him soon. Tears pressed into the corners of her eyes.

Help me, Lord! I need to rescue Matty and his grandparents.

Even though she was off duty, she still carried the full authority of a cop. Protocol was to wait for backup, but that didn't apply if she thought she had to act immediately to stop someone from dying. Not that she was about to rush in blind. Of course, if things went squirrely, she might face an internal investigation. But that was a risk she was more than ready to take, despite whatever caution her father might've advised.

"I can't wait seven minutes," Adam said,

pushing through a gate into the neighbor's backyard, Noelle following. "I have to help my son and my parents."

"Understood," she said. The backyard was long and narrow, paved by the look of it and lined with snow-covered planters. She stepped up on a bench and looked over the fence into the Jollys' yard. "I've been directed to wait for backup. And I need to remind you, as a civilian, you should not enter an active crime scene and to let law enforcement handle it."

"Duly noted," he said and stepped up on the bench beside her. "I just... I just can't... I can't do nothing."

"I know," she said. Her hand brushed his arm. "And coming around the back of the house through your neighbor's yard is smart. Give me more details. I need more intel if I'm going to be smart about this. Matty's alone in the basement?"

"Hiding in a closet," he confirmed.

"And the hostiles have gone upstairs with your parents?"

"As far as I know."

So the terrified child and the hostage elderly couple were in two different parts of the house.

Help me, Lord. I can't be in two places at once and need to stay with Adam because I need his help and direction to help save his family.

She paused for a moment as her eyes scanned the scene. "Does the laundry room have a window?"

He pointed to a small one, only about six or seven inches high and not much larger than a ventilation grate. "That one, but—"

"What's directly under it?"

"A giant laundry pile on a table. But it's too high for Matty to climb up—"

"How high's the drop?"

"Maybe a four-foot drop. Not high. But neither of us will fit through—"

"Yeah, but Liberty will." She glanced at Liberty. The dog was cross-trained in protection. "Come on."

Noelle leaped over the fence and landed low and silently in the deep snow in the Jollys' backyard. A moment later, Liberty followed, she guessed taking a running leap and using the bench as a springboard. Adam followed immediately afterward. Now she could hear the faint sound of shouting coming from what sounded like the back of the house's main floor. The even fainter sound of Matty singing quietly to himself, she guessed to calm his fear, came from the phone still in Adam's hand. She glanced at her watch. Police were five minutes out. Her heart ached.

They crawled across the snow to the window.

"Can you open it?" she asked. "And can I talk to Matty?"

He took the phone off mute and handed it to her.

"Hi, Matty?" Noelle said. "It's Noelle. Are you okay? Your daddy says you're being brave."

"Uh-huh," Matty said. Tears muffled his voice. "You're coming to save me, right?"

"Absolutely," she said. "Right now, I'm going to send Liberty in to find you. She's very good at protecting. She'll stay with you and keep you safe. Okay? She's coming now."

Adam already had the window open. She handed the phone back to Adam, then pulled the Christmas hat Matty had lent her and waved it under Liberty's nose. "Liberty. Find Matty. Protect Matty. Stay with Matty. Good dog."

Liberty woofed softly. Then she pressed her body low against the snow and crawled through the open window. She heard a soft thump followed by a shuffle, which she guessed was Liberty landing on the table and then leaping onto the floor.

Adam's gloved hand grabbed hers and squeezed it tightly. "Can she actually do this?"

"She can." Noelle nodded. "She'll place herself between Matty and danger, and she'll bark, snap and growl if anyone comes near."

"She's here!" Matty's voice filled the phone. "She found me! She's pressed up right against me. Very soft and warm."

"Thank you, God," Adam prayed softly.

"She'll keep him safe and warn us if anyone comes near him," Noelle said. "She'll give her life for your son before she lets anything happen to him. She's a pretty ferocious protector." Her eyes scanned Adam's face, then glanced down at the hand holding hers.

So was he.

"Four minutes until backup," she added. "It's almost over."

A gunshot sounded, taking out a back main floor window, sending glass cascading out into the snow. A woman's voice filled the air, screaming for help.

It was Adam's mother, and she was begging for mercy.

SIX

It was like something snapped inside Adam as he heard his mother cry out in fear. He couldn't wait for the authorities another moment. He needed to do something to save his family, now. He turned and ran for the side door, praying with every step and feeling Noelle there by his side. He reached the door, stopped and turned to Noelle. Her gaze met his, firm and reassuring.

"Your son's with Liberty," she said. "Backup is two minutes out."

"And my parents are in imminent danger," he said. "I'm going in."

"Stay behind me," she said.

They reached the door. He heard her whisper a prayer and joined in with her, their prayers mingling together as one, as he thanked God that Liberty was protecting his son. Adam yanked the door open so swiftly it was almost silent, and they stepped into his home and listened. The sound of a struggle rose from his own master bedroom.

They ran down the hall toward the door as it lay ajar in front of them and pressed their back against the wall as they glanced in the narrow gap between the door hinges. The world slowed into a tableau before his eyes, the same way it used to when he was in uniform and driving tactically under enemy fire.

His father was lying on his stomach, down on the floor, holding his hands behind his head, while a masked man stood over him, pointing a gun at him. A second armed and masked figure stood beside his mother, holding a gun to her head and barking at her to open Adam's bedroom safe. The door hinges creaked. The man holding his mother turned, his gun moving away from Irene's head as he spun toward the door. Noelle fired through the door, sending splinters flying. Her precision bullet struck the masked man by the shoulder, immobilizing the arm holding the gun and sending him falling back.

The man who'd been aiming at Fred wheeled around, but he was too late, as Adam launched himself through the doorway, grabbing his hand and forcing the gun high above their heads. The weapon fired. The bullet flew into the ceiling, sending plaster raining down around them. Adam yanked the weapon from the man's hand and then took him down to the ground and pinned him.

He glanced up. Noelle had the other masked man down on the ground and held him there. His mother helped his father to his feet, as Noelle reassured them that Liberty was guarding Matty. His eyes glanced to the clock. The whole thing had gone down in seconds. Then he heard sirens filling the air, the sound of his own front door open, voices announcing themselves as the Brooklyn K-9 Unit, and Noelle shouting back that they were in the master bedroom.

And just as suddenly as time had slowed, it sped back up again.

Men and women in uniform rushed into the room. He looked up to see Officer Morrow by his side and stepped back to let him cuff and apprehend the suspect.

"Come on." Noelle grabbed Adam's hand and he realized another officer had taken over the suspect she'd taken down. "We have to go get Matty. Liberty won't stand down without my command."

His hand tightened in hers. They ran through the house, now crowded with cops and paramedics, then pelted down the stairs and into the basement. Adam led her into the darkened laundry room, lit only by the dim glow of a night-light plugged into the wall. He crouched beside the linen closet and only then realized he was still holding Noelle's hand.

The folding door was closed and he guessed Matty had shut it after Liberty had crawled in with him.

"Matty?" he called softly. "I'm here. It's Daddy. It's safe."

Silence fell from the other side. Fear pooled in his heart. Was his son there? Was he all right? Noelle pulled her hand from his and Adam let her crouch in front of him, knowing better than to get in between a K-9 officer and her dog.

"Liberty." Noelle's voice was firm and yet somehow surprisingly soft as she slid the door open. "It's me. All done. Good..." She swallowed hard as if swallowing tears. "Good dog."

She sat back and he saw why her voice had choked. Depsite all the noise and chaos on the floor above, Matty was curled up and asleep in the nest of sleeping bags and blankets, with his chest rising and falling peacefully and his arms wrapped tightly around Liberty's body as she lay protectively in front of the little boy. Matty's face was buried deeply in her fur.

The dog's large and serious eyes looked up into Adam's eyes, as if Liberty knew that Matty was Adam's child and wanted to reassure Adam she knew how important it was that she kept him safe.

"Thank you," he told Liberty. He ran one hand along his child's cheek as he slept peacefully, nuzzled up against the brave K-9 dog protecting him. He'd let Matty nap for a little while longer, while the chaos died down upstairs.

"I just texted Morrow to let him know we have Matty and he's safe," she said.

He turned to the incredible woman crouching on the floor beside him. She slid her phone back into her pocket.

"Thank you," Adam said. "Thank you for everything. I don't know where we'd be without you."

"No problem," she said. "All in a day's work."

But it was more than that, right? At least it was for him. He took both of her hands in his, letting their fingers link through. His arms longed to hold her and pull her into his chest. He wanted to kiss her like he had in the truck.

He wanted to hand her his vulnerable and damaged heart and trust her with it.

There, in her face, he saw everything he

wanted his life and his future to be. But he'd also seen a lot of mirages in the heat of the desert sun when he'd been on the battlefield. How could he possibly know if any of what he felt for her was real? It was nothing like anything he'd ever experienced before. He prayed for wisdom.

Lord, I don't believe in love at first sight.

"I feel something for you," he admitted. "Some kind of connection. It's like a tune, a drumbeat, playing at the corner of my mind. I don't know what it is or how to turn it off. All I know is it's distracting, it's overwhelming and part of me wants it to stop."

He wanted to feel his hands back on the steering wheel of his life again, and not like someone else had grabbed it and was swerving his heart down a path he couldn't see or control.

"I'm not sure what you're trying to say," Noelle said.

Neither did he. Just like he didn't know why he was now holding her hands or why he'd kissed her back in the truck.

"My family needs me," he said.

"Yes," she said. "They do."

"And I'm not saying that any of this is your fault," he said quickly. "Not at all. You've never once done anything to put me or my family in danger—"

"I know I haven't." Noelle pulled her hands away and stood.

"But my head hasn't been in the game," Adam went on. "I've been distracted. I haven't been focused."

"I got it." Her voice chilled. She glanced at her partner and raised an eyebrow.

"Plus," he said, "you're trying to get all the overtime hours…"

"Stop." Noelle raised a hand, palm up. "Your train of thought is swerving all over the place right now, like you've got no idea where you're going, and it's giving me whiplash." Her arms crossed. "If this is your way of saying you're sorry you kissed me earlier, you can just come out and say it. You're not the first man to decide he doesn't want to be in a relationship with me."

No, that's not what he was trying to say.

But the problem was he had no idea what it was he did want to say.

"You're a really incredible person," he tried again.

I think I have a crush on you! The words shouted inside his head. *And that's scary and confusing, and I don't know what to do about it.*

"Thank you," she said curtly. "You're pretty incredible too. But I really don't want to grow any closer to a man who seems to be really confused about what he thinks of me or what kind of relationship he wants to have. Whenever a police officer fires their weapon, they have to make a report and go through an internal investigation. I'm not worried, but the fact I was off duty might complicate things. Sarge will assign a different K-9 officer to connect with your family going forward. I gave your mom my cell phone number and I'm happy to take her call if she needs something. But hopefully my unit will be able to find someone who your whole family is comfortable with."

He hesitated a moment, still crouched be-

tween where Noelle stood and Matty lay.
Then Noelle nodded to Liberty and the dog
moved to her side. Matty stirred, his eyes
opened, and a myriad of conflicting emotions battled in his face before he turned
and looked at Adam.

"Daddy!" He crawled out of the blankets
and threw his arms around Adam. "You
made it! Are the bad guys gone?"

"Yes." Adam hugged his son tightly.
"Grandma and Grandpa are safe. The police are upstairs making sure everything is
good. And I've got you."

"That was an adventure, wasn't it, Dad?"
his son said.

Adam chuckled, feeling tears form in his
throat. "Yeah, it sure was."

"Well, I should go," Noelle said. "Goodbye, guys, and Merry Christmas."

He glanced at Noelle over his son's head
and for one fleeting moment caught a
glimpse of an unexpected emotion filling
her eyes. It was like sadness or longing,
maybe even regret. All he knew was that
it made him want to pull her into the hug

and apologize for his confused and muddled heart.

Instead, he watched as the most extraordinary woman he knew turned and walked out of his life.

Traffic was still thick and the snowflakes even thicker in the dark Christmas Eve sky when Noelle finally left the Brooklyn K-9 Unit and drove home with Liberty. She hadn't minded how meticulous Sarge had been in going over every decision she'd made in how she'd responded to the hostage situation at the Jollys' house. He'd told her what to expect from the upcoming internal investigation and that she was currently on leave with pay. She liked the fact there were checks and balances in place to keep NYPD officers at the top of their game. Although she dreaded telling her folks she and Liberty were off active cases again—and that it was her own fault this time.

Besides, the longer she'd stayed there, discussing the case with Sarge, the longer she could put off thinking about her final conversation with Adam.

She liked Adam. That much she could admit to herself. She really, really liked everything about Adam. It had taken a lot of self-control to keep from pointing out it had been a very long time since she'd let anyone kiss her and she didn't know what she felt either. The *connection* as he'd called it between them confused and surprised her every bit as much as it did him.

But the last thing she needed in her life right now was an ambivalent man playing games with her heart.

Thankfully, the arrest of the two masked men at the Jollys' house had led to a major break in the case. Both perps had been members of one of the notorious drug-running gangs that the other officers in the Brooklyn K-9 Unit had been investigating. Within half an hour of their arrest, officers had gotten a warrant to raid a garage they suspected was used by the gang and had discovered a transport truck packed to the seams with pill-stuffed toys. That was the very good news. The bad news was that they'd only found the drugs after they'd apparently been transferred from the new major player on the drug scene to the gang he or she had finally decided to use as a distributor.

Who this major new dealer was, who'd apparently been shopping MDMA-filled FlupperPups around, remained a mystery. As was their connection to Adam Jolly and his family.

But that was another officer's problem now, Noelle told herself firmly, as she inched her vehicle through the snowy streets. Someone else would be sitting in their patrol car, keeping a watchful eye on the street outside the Jollys' home tonight and filling the family in on the developments in the case. Noelle and Liberty would move on to the next case and then the one after that, without her having to deal with the kind of man who intrigued her mind, flipped her heart upside down and then walked out the moment things got confusing.

No, now it was time to focus on work. And maybe give her heart some time to heal.

Her phone buzzed, letting her know a text was coming in. She pulled over to the side of the road, then glanced at the screen. It was Irene Jolly.

Hi, Noelle. It's Irene Jolly. Got a minute?

She was surprised by just how much her heart jolted to see Adam's mother's name on the screen. Noelle hadn't just liked Adam. She liked his whole family and would miss having all of them in her life.

She debated how to answer for far too long, before finally just using voice recognition to text back.

Sure. What's up?

There was no answer for a long moment. Noelle debated whether she should've left the house as quickly as she had with only a wave goodbye to Fred and Irene, as the couple stood with their arms around each other in a picture of strength, love and resilience. They'd been through a lot tonight. But it was a crime scene, Noelle was a witness, and she had to give her statement and coordinate with her fellow officers. Not to mention the fact Noelle's chest had been aching like a big and heavy weight was pressing on it.

Liberty nuzzled her hand gently as if sensing she was sad. Noelle stroked the dog's head behind her black-smudged ear. If only Liberty could tell her what to do about it.

Can we talk? Irene texted again. In person? Right now? It's important.

Noelle took a deep breath and prayed God would guide her words.

I don't know if Adam told you, she texted back, but I'm not working this case anymore. I'm actually on leave right now. Another officer will be assigned to coordinate with you.

Noelle waited for Irene's response, hoping her text hadn't come across as rude.

I know. Irene texted back. This isn't about

the case. It's a personal family thing. I don't know who to trust. And I trust you.

Irene had been really kind to her. At the very least Noelle could say goodbye to her in person, hear her out and help direct her to the right person. She owed Irene that much.

Okay, she texted back. I'm heading back to your house.

It would be awkward, but she was sure Adam would understand. Considering how busy the house was she and Adam might be able to avoid each other.

No, Irene texted. I'm actually headed to our offices/warehouse right now. Meet me there. There's something I need to show you. I'll leave the warehouse door unlocked. Meet me in the office.

Noelle's heart hammered in her chest.

No, I think it's safer to meet at the house, she texted back. The person behind all this still hasn't been caught yet. If you have to go to the warehouse wait to go with Adam or go with a cop.

Maybe she was overreacting, but she really didn't like the idea of Adam's mother going to the warehouse alone right now. Noelle waited for Irene to say okay. But there was no response. She waited another solid minute. Nothing.

Oh, no. She pulled out into traffic and turned around.

Her GPS said she'd be at the Jolly Family Charity headquarters and warehouse in eighteen minutes.

It wasn't likely this new player in the drug game would strike again so soon or be poking around the charity after it had been swept by the cops. But still, something about the idea of Irene going there alone sent shivers up her spine.

SEVEN

Adam sat alone in the darkened living room and spun his wedding ring around in his fingers. That, the gun and five hundred dollars of emergency cash was all that had been in the safe the masked men, who he now knew from police were drug dealers, had tried to force his mother to open for them. It had been half an hour since the police had left. His father had helped him board up his broken bedroom window and sweep up the plaster, door splinters and glass shards. A quick bit of plaster and paint, plus a fresh pane of glass, and it would be like nothing ever happened. Matty was already asleep in his bed.

Everything was back to normal. Except his heart.

He'd deleted Noelle's number from his

cell phone and politely evicted her from his life. Getting her out of his heart and mind though was a whole other story. He turned his old ring one way and then another in between the fingers of his injured hand, noting the places it was smooth from wear and wondering what the shape and contours of it would've been if he'd worn it several decades instead of just a few years. Then he set the ring on the table, dropped his head into his hands and prayed. *God, please give me wisdom.*

The floorboards creaked behind him and he looked up to see his dad standing there, holding his cell phone.

"Hey," Adam said. "Everything okay?"

"Pretty much," Fred said and sat down in the chair opposite him. "But what's up with Noelle?"

Adam almost laughed. Now that was the million-dollar question.

"To be honest," Adam said. "I asked her to leave because I have a crush on her."

Fred's eyebrows rose. His father glanced at the phone he was holding and his mouth opened and closed again like he was debating what to say. Then he set the phone down on the coffee table and looked at Adam. "Well, that's something. Do you want to talk about it?"

Did he? He didn't know.

"I know what you're going to say," Adam said. "You're going to ask me what Carissa would want, but I already know exactly what she'd say and that it's the same thing I'd have told her if I'd died first. I'd tell her I want her to be happy and trust her judgment on finding the right person to marry and bring into Matty's life. But that doesn't help me right now."

His father glanced at his phone again and once again Adam had the feeling this wasn't the conversation his dad had been expecting to have when he walked into the living room.

"Because you trust your own judgment less than you trust Carissa's?" his father asked. "Or because you have less of a right to be happy?"

Adam blew out a long breath. He hadn't

even gotten as far as letting himself think about happiness.

"I don't trust my heart," Adam admitted. "It's like an accelerator trying to drive me toward a future with Noelle at a reckless speed. But my brain is trying to jam the brakes on and stop. And while both parts are equally strong it feels safest to let my brain win this one. Do you think I'm making it too complicated?"

His dad crossed his arms and sat back in his chair.

"Honestly, I think you're making it way too simple," Fred said. "It's way more complicated than you're making it out to be."

Adam blinked. "What?"

"When you're a little kid, you think a car has two pedals," his dad said. "One that goes and one that stops. When you grow up, you learn a vehicle is way more complicated than that, especially the kind you drove overseas. You've got a speedometer to figure out your speed. Not to mention a really great steering wheel. You can change gears. You've got a windshield to keep the bugs from flying in your face and wind-shield wipers to clean the glass off so you can see where you want to go. And lights. Don't forget trucks have lights."

Adam laughed and leaned forward. If he didn't stop the metaphor quickly, his dad would probably try to list every vehicle part he could think of. "Yup, trucks have lights. Headlights and brake lights both."

"And high beams for bad weather," his dad added. "And turn signal lights to help the other cars around you know what you're about to do."

"Okay, okay, I get the analogy." Adam held both hands up in surrender. The irony didn't escape him. Maybe if Adam had done a better job at signaling to Noelle what he was thinking, his little speech in the basement wouldn't have run her off the road—metaphorically speaking. "I get it, I'm complicated and Noelle's complicated. People are complicated."

"Life is complicated," his dad said. "And I'm not telling you what to do. Certainly, your mother and I have a good feeling about

Noelle, and Matty likes her. All I'm saying is you're not driving around in a little kid's bumper car. You're smart enough to figure out a way forward once you get all the parts of your internal engine working together. Not to mention you can pray for guidance too, which I guess is like roadside assistance, or maybe a regular oil change and maintenance."

"Dad, stop!" Adam laughed. "No more comparing me to a car. Not that your metaphor wasn't helpful. But I think you're running it into the ground."

His dad chuckled. "Bottom line, I trust you to figure it out. I hope that helps."

"It does. Thank you."

"You're welcome," his dad said. "Now, maybe you can tell me why Noelle and Liberty are at Jolly Charity headquarters? I got an alert on my phone from that security app you installed that the motion sensors had gone off and when I looked at the camera feed it was her."

"What?" Adam sat up suddenly. "What do you mean she's at our headquarters? Is she there with other police? Are they raiding the place? Was there some kind of new lead?"

"It's just her and Liberty, and she's still in regular clothes," Fred said. He handed Adam the phone. "Even though I received a notification, the alarm didn't go off so I assumed you'd disabled it and figured something out with her?"

"No," Adam said. He glanced down at the screen. Sure enough, Noelle and Liberty were standing in the snow outside the warehouse door. Then as he watched, she pushed the door open and walked inside. The building was unlocked? How? Why? He leaped to his feet.

"Mom!" he called. "Do you know why Noelle is at our offices?"

"She is?" Irene stepped out of the kitchen, seeming to bring the scent of spices with her. "I have no idea."

"Do you have her phone number?" he asked. Why had he been so quick to delete all signs of Noelle Orton from his life?

Irene blinked. "In my contacts list. But I lost my phone in all the confusion earlier."

"Text me her number when you find it," Adam said. He pressed his phone into his dad's hands. "And keep watching the security feed from the different channels." He scooped his keys up off the table, ran for his coat and shoved his hands through the sleeves. "If anything looks wrong, call me and call the police." He stuffed his feet into his boots. "The police have a valid warrant to search the place and so it's probably nothing. But I'm heading over there, just to be safe."

And to figure out why a dozen alarm bells inside him were now ringing, clanging and warning that something was wrong.

"Hello?" Noelle called as she walked into the warehouse. The cavernous space was dimly lit and silent except for the sound of her and Liberty's footsteps on the concrete floor. "Irene?" *Please don't be here,* she prayed. *Let her have gotten my text to go home.*

Tall metal shelves of toys rose high on either side. Rows of dolls seemed to watch her with plastic eyes. She turned a corner and came face-to-face with a wall of old cardboard displays for the Jolly Family Charity. There were the Jollys over the years, starting with a much younger Fred and Irene holding a tiny baby Adam, all the way up to posters with Adam as a child, teenager and then young man in military fatigues. She turned away and headed to the office, where Irene had said to meet her.

Noelle just hoped Adam's mother didn't want to talk to her about her son.

Walking through the dimly lit warehouse, she realized just how vast the space was. A shiver ran down her spine, warning her of something but she couldn't tell if it was a police thing or something in her heart. She ran her hand over the back of Liberty's neck. The dog was tense.

Okay, so it wasn't just her.

Help me, Lord. I don't want to be that rookie who calls the higher-ups just be-

cause I arranged to meet a nice lady who had quite an ordeal earlier tonight.

Then again, better safe than sorry. She texted Raymond.

Hey, do you have a second? Irene Jolly asked me to meet at her office to talk about something personal. I told her not to go there alone and that I'd meet her at home. But she didn't respond. I'm not sure if she got my text and maybe I'm just being overcautious. But something feels off.

A light flickered on ahead and above her, sending a soft golden glow over the warehouse. Noelle looked up to see the offices. They were a freestanding two-story block of rooms in the middle of the warehouse. The room that was now lit up was on the second floor. A person was silhouetted behind the shades.

Her phone buzzed. It was Irene.

I'm in my office. Can you see me?

The person behind the blinds waved. Noelle waved back and then texted, I can see you!

Noelle turned and walked toward the glowing light ahead. Liberty whimpered slightly. Okay, so Noelle might be relieved, but it seemed her partner was still sure something was wrong. She stopped and turned to Liberty. The dog's ears were perked up and her snout was practically straining as she sniffed the air.

"You smell something?" Noelle asked. "Okay. Show me. Let's go."

Liberty barked, a short, sharp sound like a starting pistol. Then she tugged on the leash, taking off running in between a row of toys to her right, as Noelle jogged after her. Her heartbeat quickened. Her phone buzzed in her pocket. Then Liberty stopped short in front of a shelf and Noelle looked up to see row upon row of FlupperPups. Her heart stopped. No, it couldn't be. The Jollys' warehouse had been cleared of anything suspicious—including all Flupper-Pups.

She looked at Liberty. "Are you sure?"

Liberty barked again and pointed her nose to one specific FlupperPup that sat almost at her eye level, as if to say, *This one Noelle! Check this one!*

It was a black lab with a red bow. Noelle reached for it, picked it up and shook it slightly. It rattled. She prayed.

Help me, Lord. What's going on? What have I found?

She set the dog down as her phone buzzed in her pocket with a call. She glanced at the screen. It was Raymond. She answered.

"Just who I need to talk to right now," she said. "I've got a situation on my hands. I'm at Jolly Charity headquarters but Liberty alerted to something. She followed the scent and led me to what I'm pretty sure is another FlupperPup full of MDMA pills. Now, I'm not on duty, I'm actually on leave, but I picked it up, and judging by the weight distribution and rattling, there are definitely pills inside. Plus, Liberty is convinced and her nose is never wrong."

Raymond took in a sharp breath.

"Rewind a second." His voice was sharp

and urgent. "Irene Jolly contacted you and asked you to meet her at her warehouse?"

"Yes," she confirmed. "We've developed a bit of a friendship. Cookies and an invitation to Christmas dinner, that kind of thing. She said she wanted to talk to me about something personal. I'm sorry if I should've cleared it with someone. But I thought the Jollys' warehouse and offices had been swept by the K-9 team and were found clean."

"They were," Raymond said, his voice tight and urgent. "But the Jolly family and staff have not been given clearance to re-enter the property until the twenty-sixth."

"So Irene shouldn't be here," Noelle said.

"No one should be there," Raymond said. "And there definitely shouldn't be any FlupperPups testing positive for MDMA."

So, what was it doing here? What had she just walked into?

"What do I do?" Noelle asked.

"Stay there," Raymond said. She could tell by the jangle of keys and dog tags he was already heading to the door and taking Abby with him. "Secure the package. Wait for me outside. And if you see anyone, call me."

"Drop the phone. Now!" The voice was loud, male and cold, and seemed to echo in the warehouse around her. She looked up. A heavyset man in a puffy jacket was standing at the end of the row. He was in his late fifties with graying dark hair and it took her a moment to recognize him from the case files.

It was Lou Shmit, the owner of Dotty's Toys.

There was nowhere to hide. He was too far away to disarm.

"Get down on the ground," Lou said. He aimed the red dot on the scope of his most certainly illegal semi-automatic right between Liberty's eyes. "Right now. Or I'll kill you both before you can even flinch."

Adam drove as quickly as he safely could through New York's dark and snowy streets. Something was wrong. He didn't know what. All he knew was a sense of urgency was beating through his heart too loudly to ignore. Why had Noelle gone to the warehouse alone?

Would she have called him first if he hadn't pushed her out of his life?

Lord, please make sure she is all right.

His phone rang from a number he didn't recognize.

He answered using his truck's hands-free. "Hello. Adam Jolly here."

"Mr. Jolly. This is Officer Raymond Morrow."

"Where's Noelle?" Adam asked. "What's going on? Is she okay?" Traffic grew thick ahead. "Why is she at my charity's headquarters?"

"She said your mother texted and asked to meet her there."

He took a sharp breath. "That wasn't my mom. Irene is home. She said she lost her phone earlier today, and I'm guessing it was stolen or pickpocketed. I don't know."

He heard what sounded like Officer Morrow praying under his breath and typing at the same time.

Adam prayed too. The fear grew deeper as the snow thickened outside his vehicle.

"I've already called it in and I'm on the way to your headquarters," Raymond said.

"I'm on my way there too," Adam said.

"As a civilian, I have to advise you to let police handle this."

"Got it," Adam said. "I'll be there in two."

"Again, keep a safe distance. Should be there in eight."

Adam turned another tight corner, cut through the narrow gap between two buildings and then his own warehouse came into view. He pulled into the parking lot. The warehouse's loading bay door began to open. Then a white van shot through so quickly the roof bashed hard against the raising door, denting the door and scuffing the van.

"Morrow!" he shouted into the phone. "We have a situation!"

He sped toward the van, locking it in his sights. He was going to ram it. He had to. He couldn't let it make it out of the parking lot. Not if there was even the smallest possibility Noelle was trapped inside.

The van swerved and as he watched the back door swung open and a mass of blond fur flew out, tumbling and rolling in the snow.

It was Liberty!

Someone had thrown her from the van, and he was about to drive right into her.

"Help me, Lord!" He shouted a prayer, hit the brakes and swerved hard, skidding across the icy ground, just feet away from where the dog had been tossed into the snow. The truck stopped and Adam looked up to see Liberty pulling herself up to her feet. The dog's legs tensed, as if ready to sprint after the departing van, and dispelled any doubt he had that Noelle was inside. He threw the driver's side door open.

"Liberty!" Adam shouted and patted the side of his seat. "Come on! Get in! We'll chase Noelle together!"

Liberty turned and ran for him. Her coat was dirty from the snow and she seemed to be limping slightly. But as he bent down to pick her up, Liberty leaped, bouncing off his legs and landing in the passenger seat. *Okay, then.* He slammed the door. Liberty's snout brushed his jaw as if thanking him, and then she barked as if ordering him to drive.

"Yeah, I got it." He looked up to where the van was merging into traffic ahead. "That van's got Noelle and we're going to get her back."

He put the truck in Drive and sped after the van, shouting details to Officer Morrow about the vehicle's make and model, damage from the door, license plate, the direction it was heading, that Adam now had Liberty—and the fact he was certain Noelle was inside the van.

The van had merged into traffic and seemed to be heading toward the docks. Adam kept it in his sights, cutting through parking lots and driving over curbs to keep from losing it. The van's driver grew more reckless, surging over barriers, running red lights and darting down one-way streets the wrong way. He could hear Liberty barking encouragement in his ear and Officer Morrow telling him law enforcement would intercept the van ahead. Adam clenched his jaw and prayed as he inched closer and closer.

He wouldn't let it out of his sight. He would not let it get away.

Then the van swerved into an industrial parking lot, vast and empty, dotted with piles of snow left from a snowplow.

It was time. Adam shifted gear, hit the accelerator and sped toward the van, forcing the speedometer higher and higher, as he waited for the exact right moment. Then he struck, smashing into the corner of the van's bumper and sending it spinning to the right, flying across the ice and into a snowbank in a perfectly controlled crash, with the precision of a hockey player smacking the puck into the net. The sound of smashing metal filled the air. A plume of snow and dirt rose above the van.

Adam fumbled for his seat belt, leaped from his vehicle and ran across the lot with Liberty by his side.

A gunshot rang out inside the van.

Adam stopped short, his hand instinctively grabbing Liberty's collar and pulling her to his side. Panicked prayers filled his heart, choking his ability to breathe.

Noelle! Please, Lord, I need her to be okay.

The van's back door fell open and Noelle leaped out into the snow, landing on the balls of her feet. Her hair fell in a tangled mess around her face. Her clothes were battered and torn. A smoking semi-automatic was clutched in her hand. But as her eyes locked on his, the strength and determination in their green depths took his breath away. His own name moved silently on her lips.

"Adam, it's Lou," Noelle said, as she found her voice. "Lou Shmit. He's injured in the van and handcuffed. It's over."

Questions tumbled through his mind as he ran for her, hearing Liberty's urgent woof as the dog outpaced him. Police sirens filled the air. Liberty reached Noelle first, barely giving her time to set the weapon down before Liberty leaped into her arms, the dog's paws landing on her shoulders.

Noelle hugged her partner. Adam reached Noelle and to his surprise Noelle threw her arms around him and hugged him tightly. And for one long moment, he let himself hold her, feeling her heart beating against his as he breathed her in.

"It was Lou Shmit this whole time," Noelle said. "He's the mysterious new drug lord. He kidnapped me in the warehouse, hoping he could force me to tell him how to get around the K-9 dogs' capabilities. I managed to kick one of the back doors open and told Liberty to jump but then the door swung shut and I was stuck. When you forced us to crash, I got free, wrestled him for the gun and shot him in the leg. He'll be okay."

"But are you okay?" he asked.

"I am." She nodded and he felt her hair brush his face, before she pulled back and looked him in the eyes. "Thank you for saving my life."

"It was a team effort—"

"Your mom—"

"She's home safe. Someone took her

phone. We're not even sure when. Likely pickpocketed or stolen by one of the dealers at the event earlier tonight—"

Police vehicles and ambulances surged around them. The cavalry had arrived. Her hand brushed the side of his face and he felt hundreds of words he wanted to speak fill his mind. He wanted to tell her he was sorry and how scared he'd been at the thought of losing her. Instead, he pushed his cell phone into her hands.

"It's Officer Morrow," he said. "We've been on the phone."

"Thank you," she said and took the phone.

"I'm so sorry," he whispered.

"Tell me later," she said. "When we have the time to just sit and talk, away from all this." Then she leaned forward and her lips brushed his cheek in a kiss. "And tell your mother I'm coming for Christmas lunch."

Then she pressed the phone to her ear and he turned toward the emergency vehicles.

EIGHT

It was Christmas Day and the late morning sunshine filtered through the snow that fell faint and dazzling like glitter outside the Jolly family home. Adam was in the living room, tidying the brightly colored wrapping paper scattered around the floor from where it had fallen when they'd opened presents. The smell of turkey and gravy cooking came from the kitchen, along with the happy voices of his parents and Matty.

He and Noelle had barely spoken and hadn't had a moment alone since the emergency vehicles had converged on the scene of the crash the night before. He'd given multiple statements to police, seen Lou rolled away, ranting angrily on a stretcher, and even relented to a quick look over by a paramedic himself. Then he'd headed home where two hours of gift wrapping had awaited him. He'd told his parents Noelle and Liberty were coming for Christmas, placed the presents under the tree and reassured his mom that she had indeed set the cinnamon buns for breakfast to bake in the bread maker overnight. Then he'd finally tumbled into bed shortly after midnight only to be woken up by an excited Matty bouncing on his bed at six in the morning. There'd then been Christmas stockings and warm cinnamon buns with butter, followed by family church and opening presents.

Yet, somehow, it hadn't quite felt like Christmas, until the moment he heard the crunch of tires in the snow outside his house and looked out to see Noelle and Liberty walking up the driveway. He watched as Noelle whispered something in Liberty's ear and then he opened the door, Liberty barreling through.

"Matty's in the kitchen!" he told Liberty, as her snout brushed his leg briefly, before bounding past him into the kitchen where Matty greeted her with glee.

Then Adam slid his feet into his boots and stepped outside to meet Noelle. There was a familiar-shaped and gift-wrapped box in her hands. His eyebrows rose. "You brought a FlupperPup?"

"It's for Matty," she said. "I know Irene already got him one, but I thought these two could be friends. It's a yellow Lab. I used some black fabric paint to paint a black smudge on her ear to match Liberty's."

Gratitude surged in Adam's heart. How had he possibly met a woman as amazing and thoughtful as her?

"He'll love it," Adam said. "It's perfect. You're...you're perfect."

He hesitated, feeling his arms ache to hug her, but not wanting to squish the package in her hands.

"I need to tell you that we found one more drug-filled FlupperPup," she said. "It was in Quentin's apartment. You were right that he had nothing to do with Lou Shmit's drug-smuggling enterprise. It just happened to be the only FlupperPup in the toy shipment for your first event on the twenty-third. When he saw how Matty made a beeline for it and picked it up, Quentin set it aside, to ask you if he could give it to him. Then he forgot about it. I think he's planning on calling you later, but didn't want to interrupt Christmas morning. But that explains the mystery of why Liberty sensed trace amounts of drugs on Matty at the mall."

"I'm really thankful that Liberty did," he said. "I shudder to think what would've happened to all of us if she hadn't led you to us."

A smile filled her face. "I'm really thankful too."

His hand slid down and squeezed her free one.

"Come inside," he said. "Everyone's looking forward to seeing you, lunch will be ready soon and we have cinnamon buns left over from breakfast if you can't wait."

Besides, he'd been in such a hurry to greet her he'd forgotten to put on his coat.

"One moment," she said. "You said a lot

of words to me yesterday and I have something I want to say to you."

She took a deep breath and he felt something tighten in his chest.

"I like you, Adam," she said. "I really, really like you. I get why you're scared because this is all new to me too. I've never met someone I felt this way about before. Which is why…"

Her words trailed off and she took a deep breath, her eyes closing as if she were praying silently. Then she opened them again and took another step toward him until he could feel the warmth of her against his chest.

"Which is why I want us to be friends, just for a while," she said. "I want to get to know your parents and your son. I want to get to know you and I want you to get to know me, until we're both ready for something more."

Something rumbled deep in his chest. He looked down at their linked hands. Then his other hand brushed her cheek.

"There's nothing I want more for Christmas," he said, "than to get to know you better."

"Me too," she said softly.

Two months later, faded red and pink construction paper Valentine hearts covered his living room mantel where the Christmas garland had been. Adam stood at the front window and watched as Matty and Liberty charged around the melted remnants of their Christmas snowmen, skidding on the tufts of grass from the first thaw of spring, which Adam knew would be covered up soon enough by a fresh burst of snow.

Then he turned to where Noelle sat on the couch and his heart soared with thanksgiving for how their relationship had grown, day by day, week by week, meal by meal and conversation by conversation, as slowly they'd gotten to know each other. She'd passed her internal police investigation with flying colors and was back to working long hours on new high-profile drugs cases with Liberty and the rest of their team. But she always made time for Adam and his family. And as for right now, in this quiet moment alone, he had her full attention, and she had his.

"I have a surprise," he said. He pulled his guitar from its place by the couch, then sat down on the coffee table opposite her and started to strum. "I've been practicing. It's slow going, but I'm getting there."

For a long moment, he sat there, his knees bumping hers and singing under his breath as he played one of the first songs he'd learned as a teenager.

When he finished, Noelle leaned toward him.

"You have no idea how extraordinary you are, do you, Adam?" she asked.

"Funny," he said and set the guitar down. "I feel the same way about you."

Her hand brushed his jaw.

"Is it okay if I tell you I love you?" she asked.

"Very okay," he said. "Because I'm so very in love with you too, Noelle. I love everything about you. How you care, how you push yourself and who you're striving to be. I love how you are with my parents and Matty. I miss you every moment you're not around and I'm so unbelievably happy when you're near me. You make me feel like the richest man alive."

Her hand slid around the back of his neck. "I'm ready to be more than friends, if you are."

He took her face in his hands and thanked God for blessing him with this extraordinary woman.

"I'm ready to ask you to marry me," he confessed.

"And I'm ready to say yes to that," she said.

A grin turned at the corner of his mouth. "Noelle, will you please marry me and be my wife?"

"Of course I will."

Then he pulled her into his arms and kissed her deeply, knowing without a shadow of a doubt he was holding the woman he was going to spend the rest of his life with.

* * * * *

Dear Reader,

I've always loved dogs. I have two in my life right now, one of which was rescued from a shelter and the other was adopted from a family friend. They're both tiny and have such different personalities. One will only ever sleep next to my head and the other only my feet. One furiously chases squirrels with a focused determination. The other happily bounces around during the chase with no real direction or idea of what she's supposed to be doing.

I really love the K-9 Love Inspired Suspense series and feel really honored to be a part of them, especially as I was a fan of some of the other authors in the series before I was even published. My fictional dogs are every bit as real to me as the human characters, including Harry the precocious Canadian husky, Queenie the sweet Texan electronics detection dog, Garfunkel the protective Malinois and now Liberty, who my fellow authors did such a wonderful job of describing before I wrote this story about her and Noelle.

For many of us, this has been a hard and tricky year and for some this Christmas might not look the way we're used to. As Adam tells Noelle, there's no one right way to celebrate Christmas. My prayer is that wherever this finds you, and whomever you celebrate with, you're surrounded by love, faith, joy and hope.

Thank you as always for sharing this journey with me,
Maggie